WILD C█████████S

Wild Cow Ranch 6

Natalie Bright
Denise F. McAllister

Wild Cow Christmas
Natalie Bright
Denise F. McAllister

Paperback Edition
CKN Christian Publishing
An Imprint of Wolfpack Publishing
5130 S. Fort Apache Rd. 215-380
Las Vegas, NV 89148

cknchristianpublishing.com

Paperback ISBN: 978-1-63977-021-2
Ebook ISBN: 978-1-63977-020-5
LCCN 2021950484

WILD COW CHRISTMAS

Dedication

To the memory of Clayton Matthew. Precious son, forever in our hearts.
~NB

Since this is a Christmas story, thank you to God for giving us the first Christmas story. "And she brought forth her firstborn Son, and wrapped Him in swaddling clothes, and laid Him in a manger, because there was no room for them in the inn." –NKJV
~DM

Chapter One

Carli

The annual Creek County equine sale was under-way at the fairgrounds, about forty-five minutes from the Wild Cow Ranch. Newlyweds Carli and Lank Torres arrived late, picking their way through the metal bleachers to find empty seats.

"Angie and Colton are coming too, right?" Lank asked his wife.

She nodded her head. "Yes, we need four spots."

They walked past two empty spaces on the end and climbed higher.

On the main level a pipe-railed fence encircled a dirt floor. At the back of the ring, raised high and eye-level with the stands, a group of people gathered with laptops and video screens. The auctioneer stood in the middle wearing a Silverbelly hat, black sports coat, and light blue tie. Spotters were stationed on the outside of the ring and some in the aisle higher up in the stands so they could catch everyone's bid.

Settled next to Lank, Carli looped her arm in his and watched the spirited blue roan that pranced around the show ring. It was an unusual gray with black legs, mane, and tail.

"This filly is two years old and ready to be trained. She'll make a fine ranch horse or trail ride competitor. Open your hearts and wallets, folks. Proceeds go to the local women's shelter. Opening bid is $500." The auctioneer began the rapid-fire cadence as the price rose higher.

"She's pretty," said Lank.

"Too spirited for what I'm wanting," Carli replied with a shake of her head.

"Sold!" the auctioneer shouted. People clapped and the new owner paid at the desk.

The next horse up might've been a draft horse cross. Sturdy, muscled, but not the height of a Clydesdale. Flaxen mane and tail, nice to look at. The audience got a little excited and the bids started flying. Carli passed on this one, and the next three groups also.

"You don't see anything you like?" asked Lank.

She had particular needs and it was hard to explain. She would know the right ones when she saw them. Definitely quiet, mature, slow even. Bomb-proof, horse people called it. For therapeutic riding, she didn't want to worry about the horse. The rider was her number one concern and priority.

Carli waved across the sea of people. "Oh, look. There's Angie."

Her friend Angie Olsen stood at the doorway, scanning the crowd in the stands. Behind her was Lank's best friend Colton Creacy. Carli stood and waved again until Angie saw her. She looked stunning as usual, her long blonde hair falling on either side of her heart-shaped face. Her outfit was color-coordinated, and Angie looked like a model in a western fashion catalog.

Her friend raised an arm and waved back.

"Sold! Eight-fifty to the young lady in the turquoise hat." Angie froze and with a look of horror on her face turned towards the front counter. She chatted to the spotter who stood the closest to her, smiled, and shook her head.

Carli and Lank couldn't help but laugh.

"You should have seen the look on your face." Carli laughed as Angie got closer. "Do you know what you just bought?"

"I think an older Quarter Horse, maybe twelve. I'll give you a good price if you want him for the riding school." Angie wiggled her eyebrows.

"Always the businesswoman," laughed Carli. "Fine. What'll you take for him?"

"Nine hundred," said Angie without hesitation.

"You bumped it up fifty bucks."

"All right. Since we're friends and all, I'll donate him, but you'll have to train him. I don't have the time."

"That's my plan. Winter them and then come spring I'll start training. I'm hoping to find older horses that are good around kids." Carli turned her attention to the ring again where a sorrel-colored horse was being shown. Reddish body, mane, and tail, with a smidgen of white on one fetlock or ankle.

"Oh, he might work. I wish we could sit closer." Carli watched the horse trot at the encouragement of the handler. It looked sound. She heard the auctioneer say the mare was around ten years old and very docile. "Lank, she'd be good for the riding program. I'm going to raise my card."

"Okay," he said. "If you're sure. Now you'll have two new ones."

She quickly got the attention of the spotter near her, and he conveyed her bid to the auctioneer. There were four or five other people interested in this horse, all with their arms raised. It was the job of the spotters to make sure the order of bidders was conveyed and acknowledged. No one wanted a fight.

"Eight fifty, nine, nine-fifty over there. Going once . . ."

"Oh, Lank, I really want her."

The spotter nearest them gave Carli a look and encouraging thumbs up asking if she'd go higher.

Carli raised her card again.

"We have one thousand for this sweet mare. Going once, going twice . . ."

Seemed the others backed out. Carli's stomach flipped.

"Going three times. Sold to the lady in the stands! Bidder number 201." The spotter made an oversized gesture as he pointed a finger at her.

Angie reached around Lank and patted Carli's shoulder. "You go, girl! Got yerself another horse. Paid more than I did though." Angie smirked.

"The way I see it," Carli said, "I paid one thousand for this one. And I got another horse valued at eight-fifty for nothing because of your donation. So, if I divide the thousand by two horses, it's like I only paid five hundred for each. I'd say that was a pretty good bargain, wouldn't you?" Carli beamed a big smile.

Colton, the real joker of the bunch, and Angie's boyfriend, let out a big laugh and jabbed Angie. "Guess she got you, hon!" She glared at him.

"The real winners are the kids in the riding program. Now we'll have two new horses. And I truly thank you for your donation." Carli reached around Lank and patted Angie's shoulder.

"You're welcome, friend." Angie smiled.

They made their way out of the stands towards the exit, Colton following Lank to bring the trailer around, and Carli followed Angie to the office to pay. With that done, she and Angie walked outside to hand the receipts to the pen supervisor and then turned to see Lank talking to a young girl. Standing with her hands on her back, a very pregnant stomach cast a shadow over her feet. Since Lank didn't offer introductions, Carli introduced herself.

"Hi, I'm Carli."

"We've met," the girl said. "At the Olsen's party right after you moved here. I'm Mandy Milam." A half-smile etched her face but didn't reach her eyes.

"When's the baby due?" Angie asked.

Carli vaguely remembered the pretty blonde, who even now couldn't tear her eyes away from Lank. With unshed tears glowing in her eyes, she looked at Angie. "In a few weeks."

"Well, congratulations," Carli said with a forced smile.

"Not really," replied Mandy as she turned her attention back to the men. "It's really great seeing you guys. I've got to get back inside and sort out these sales tickets. Come by and see me. We can talk about old times. We had some wild parties, didn't we?"

Carli didn't miss the fingertips resting on her husband's arm.

Lank ignored the question as Carli glared at him. They said goodbyes, Angie offered a good luck, and then they waited for the cowboys to run Carli's horses up to the front. Lank jumped in the pickup truck and backed it up to the loading chute. Angie stood next to Carli while they waited.

"Didn't she used to have platinum blonde hair? I think I do remember her at one of your family's barbecues."

"Yes, very blonde. She and Lank dated for a time, as I'm sure you heard."

"Heard about it, but he's mine now." Carli smiled. "There's something else I wanted to talk to you about."

"Shoot," said Angie.

"I'm hoping to bring back the Christmas celebration that Grandma Jean started years ago," Carli said. "Decorations, cookies, and the annual Open House."

"That's a wonderful idea. We never missed it. Be sure and let us know how we can help. I remember all the Boy Scout and Girl Scout troops planned their holiday field trips out to the Wild Cow. Several churches were on a schedule to sing carols. It was such a fun day."

"That's what I hear." Carli smiled. She'd come a long way since she first inherited the ranch and moved to Texas. Her grandparents were deceased, she never got to know them, and now she wanted to bring back some of their traditions.

"Have you decided when to have it?"

"I'm looking at the third Saturday in December."

"Your grandma always had it the first weekend but that'll work."

"I just barely recovered from the wedding and reception, and then Thanksgiving is in a couple of days, so we need a little time to catch our breath. I haven't really talked much about the planning to Buck and Lola yet. They know I want to do it though."

Angie laughed. "With Lola's organizing skills, she'll have everybody on board within no time."

"That's what I'm counting on," said Carli. "I have a lot to do and less than one month, plus get these new horses settled in for spring training."

"Famous last words. Come spring you'll be knocked up and painting the spare room in pastels."

Carli shook her head. "Nope. I have no aspirations to have any babies of my own. My kids are my riding school clients and our remuda of horses. That's my family, plus the Wild Cow Ranch too, of course. The kids will take all my attention, and then I can send them home to their parents. It's a win-win."

"Mmmm huh," muttered Angie.

"I don't have room for anything else. These horses will need my undivided attention this winter. I want them healthy by spring and ready to work."

Angie did not reply.

"Stop looking at me like that," said Carli. "I have this all planned and it's going to work out great. You'll see."

With a quick hug for her friend, and promises to double date within the next week, Carli waved one more goodbye to Angie. As she and Lank drove away, the strawberry blonde caught her eye again. Mandy leaned against a dented, faded blue car, the backseat cluttered with clothing, plastic containers, and unidentifiable junk. The girl took a long drag from a cigarette, her shoulders slumped forward in utter exhaustion. As she glanced up, Carli couldn't help but notice a deep frown etched her face and eyes sharp with anguish.

Chapter Two

Mandy

Mandy Milam watched the pickup truck and trailer drive away; the silhouette of a strong jaw and cowboy hat always tugged at her heart. That cowboy had been one of the biggest mistakes she had ever made. She remembered how he used to look at her with soft eyes, goofy in love and full of promise for their future. She had been too young and too stupid to recognize the kind of man he was. Solid. Kind-hearted. Seeing Lank Torres at the sale barn with his new wife reminded her that there were good men left in this world. They weren't all lying pigs.

The proof of her next biggest mistake was growing in her belly. Remembering the words of her grandmother, "Out of every storm comes a rainbow," she had decided to move onward and not look back. She could hardly wait to meet him. She'd do anything for her son.

"Mandy!"

The shout from inside the sale barn came from her boss who was a decent guy but treated her like one of the cowhands instead of a very pregnant young lady. Make that girl. She definitely was not a lady, although her mother had tried.

"Right here," she answered as she trudged towards the entrance, every deliberate step a slow effort in keeping her balance. She couldn't see her feet, and she had this uncanny fear of toppling to the ground. Surely this kid would decide to grace her with his presence soon. How much more growing could he need?

"Mandy," Calvin called again, curter and more impatient. He didn't realize how utterly slow a pregnant girl needed to walk.

"What? I'm here," she answered.

"This gentleman says his ticket is calculated wrong. Can you help him?"

"Certainly. What seems to be the problem, sir?"

The old man had picked out ten heifer calves, grade five at the most. They weren't the top of the stock that had been run through the sale barn today, but they would get the best attention and care. Kindness reflected in his eyes. The auction was the highlight of his entire week. He always sat in the same spot, third row from the bottom, second seat, and this week he had made several bids. Today was probably the most exciting day of his entire month by the way he insisted that there was a problem. He had convinced himself that he had caught them at something. She argued with him for a good half hour over a nonexistent math error, but her back got to hurting so bad she had to put a stop to it.

"Look, Mr. Parker. I can see what you're saying and why you are concerned, but you know we charge a small fee. Here's my run sheet. Here is the ending bid listed on each heifer, and here is the average weight, and what you paid along with the fee. Let's go over the math again."

This time she convinced him, and her calculator tape must have matched the math he did in his head. She stapled the printed calculations to his receipt as he wrote a check, which seemed to take forever. She watched transfixed while he carefully wrote every letter with a trembling, veined hand.

"Thank you, sir. You picked out a good-looking bunch of animals today. Hand this to the loaders after you get your trailer backed up. They will need this lot number and then they'll bring your new cows around. We'll see you next week."

He shuffled out the door but stopped at one of the tables in the café. Mandy watched him through the cloudy glass that separated the office from the front lobby and dining area. He showed the group of men his receipt and her calculator tape. This could go on until nightfall. She grinned to herself.

"You are so good with the difficult ones," said Candace, part-time help for Tuesday sale days.

"They're harmless. This is the highlight of their entire week. Tuesday auction days are important to this town."

"Mandy. The computer froze. I can't print this ticket." The boss's young daughter, Vicki, helped them on sale days too.

"Hang on, I'm coming." Mandy waddled to the other end of the long counter and sat down at the computer. At least she was off her feet for a while. Within minutes she had it working again. "All set."

"Thank you," said Vicki. "What is my dad going to do when you take maternity leave? This place won't survive."

A slight wave of panic washed through her at the comment. What was she going to do for baby food and diapers if she took maternity leave? She couldn't afford to take the time off, and where was she going to put a newborn?

Instead of crumpling to the floor and screaming her head off, she gave Vicki a false smile. "You girls can handle it until I'm back."

"Mandy! I need you to deliver a load of cows for this gentleman." Behind Calvin followed a stocky young man about her age in dusty overalls and a sweat-stained ball cap that read "Thank a Farmer". Who wore overalls anymore?

"Okay," she said, as she grabbed a pad and pen. "Give me the directions."

So many miles on highway number whatever and then turn at the big oak, and so many miles on the dirt road to the ranch entrance, and then so many miles to the right. She'd see a set of pens on the hill. She barely listened.

"Would you like me to draw a map?" he asked.

"That's a good idea." She stretched her aching back.

"You're a girl," he said.

"Yes, I am. You are very observant."

"I mean they have you driving a rig full of cows, instead of one of the boys?"

"I just do whatever needs to be done, sir. In looking at your ticket, I'm assuming you brought a trailer too, or will I need to make two trips?"

"My hitch broke and I haven't had a chance to weld it back together. So, yes, you'll need to make two trips, if that's all right?"

"I can do that." She had worked through lunch

and now it looked like she'd miss dinner too. Maybe she could grab something left over from the lunch run on her way out the door.

"I'll get the twenty-foot gooseneck hitched for you, Mandy," said Calvin as he passed through to his back office.

"We're all set then." She glanced down at the ticket. "Mr. Phineas Shelton."

She tried to stifle a giggle but failed.

"It's just Phin."

"You're not named after the cartoon character then?"

"Great-grandfather," he said. "He was British."

"Ahhh, well, Mr. Shelton, I'll see you at your place in a few and we thank you for your business."

With a heavy sigh Mandy waddled to the ladies' room and passed back through the kitchen, grabbing a bottle of juice and a biscuit leftover from breakfast. That would have to tide her over for now. The sooner she got on the road, the sooner this day would be done, and she could get off her feet.

"Drive safe, Mandy."

"Sure thing, boss."

Chapter Three

Mandy

Mandy had been driving along the dirt road forever, miles of dry grass stretched in all directions for as far as she could see. Not a tree in sight and the perfect place to grow a herd of cows. She loved the stark beauty of the Texas Panhandle. For a brief moment she admired the cerulean blue sky, but the kid was bouncing on her bladder. She just had to make a pit stop. A nine-month pregnant girl squatting on the side of the road wouldn't be a pretty sight, but in the middle of nowhere, the odds of anybody driving up were slim to none.

Pulling to a stop, the cows grew suddenly restless and jostled back and forth, causing the trailer to rock. For privacy she opened the passenger cab door next to the bar ditch. That would have to do. She didn't hear the other pickup truck until a cloud of dust rolled over her.

"Are you all right?"

Boots crunched on the gravel road and then she saw a cowboy hat in her peripheral vision over the hood.

"Stop!" she screeched.

"Sorry." The footsteps halted.

Midway to a standing position, with her pants almost pulled up, she lost her balance. Toppling to one side she rolled into the bar ditch like a beached seal until she came to a rest on her back.

"Are you okay?" The man from the sale barn rushed towards her.

"Do I look like I'm okay? What kind of stupid question is that?" She heard the sarcasm and anger in her voice which caused her cheeks to burn with embarrassment. He was only trying to help. Her clumsiness wasn't his fault, and yet his presence irritated the fool out of her.

"Let me help you up."

"Shut your eyes," she demanded.

"Okay, but I have to get to you first." He hurried closer and dutifully shut both eyes while he put his hands under her armpits. A soft grunt escaped from his lips as he lifted her off the ground.

"Keep 'em closed." Mandy quickly tugged up her stretchy top pants and yanked her shirt back in place to cover her belly. "Okay."

He opened his eyes and met her stare with a grin. The awkwardness of the situation hung in the air for several minutes. "You're almost to my place. If you'll follow, we'll get you unloaded."

With a nod of her head, she climbed back into her truck. Her cheeks burned hot, and blood pounded her temples. Not only had she acted like a clumsy ox, but she then lashed out and blamed him for it. If he filed a complaint with Calvin, she would lose her job for sure.

As she pulled closer to a set of pipe rail pens, he

motioned for her to back the long trailer up to one end of the alley. She nodded. Parked and hopped out.

"Wow. You back really good for a girl."

She bristled but held back a retort. He didn't need more fuel for the fire, in case he called Calvin. Instead, she swallowed her pride. "I'm really sorry I snipped at you back there."

He unlatched the back-trailer gate and looked at her through the slats. "It's no problem." Amusement danced in his eyes.

She couldn't hold back her grin. "Did you see anything?"

He laughed. "If I did, I wouldn't admit to it."

With a long pole and flag, he eased the cows down the alley and shut the gate behind them. They were quick to find the water and drank thirstily, as if they had been on the highway for hours.

"Ready to get that second load?" he asked.

"Sure. I'll be back as quick as I can, Mr. Shelton," Mandy said.

"Is it okay if I jump in and ride with you for the second load? And call me Phin."

"I guess so."

They bumped along the dirt road in silence. Mandy wished she would have asked to use his restroom before they left. If she made it back to the sale barn without stopping, it would be a miracle.

"When's the baby due?"

She glanced over to see if he really wanted to know or if he was just making small talk. To her surprise he was looking at her with a questioning glance. He waited.

If he had had his nose buried in his cell phone, she would have refused to talk the rest to the way.

Insincere people really bugged her.

He still waited, looking at her without blinking.

"Uh, a couple weeks. It's hard to say with the first one, so they tell me."

"Should you go to the doctor, after . . . you know." Suddenly he seemed uneasy.

"After what?"

"After you rolled into the ditch. Nothing hurt on ya, is it?"

Mandy giggled. She must have looked ridiculous. She hadn't felt like giggling in a long time. It felt good. "Tell me about your farm, Mr. Shelton."

"Phin, please. I run about one hundred head, and I grow hay grazer. We have pigs and chickens. We do a little bit of everything around here."

"We?" she asked.

"My parents and I. My brother and his wife help when they can."

"You still live with your parents?" That escaped her lips before she could stop it.

"No. Actually, we have separate houses."

"Sounds like you have a big operation then." She had never noticed him before and she knew all the regulars.

"Does your husband work at the sale barn too?" he asked.

Swallowing the lump in her throat and ever cautious to not give away any of her secrets, she hesitated. On second thought, what did it matter? She would probably never talk to him again.

"There is no husband. I'm raising this baby on my own." She let out a whoosh of air after she said it. Telling the truth was so liberating.

"Oh." Was all he managed as a response.

They drove the remainder of the way in a longer silence this time. She backed up to the loading chute at the sale barn, and before he got out of the vehicle, he looked at her and asked, "Can I grab us some food for the return trip with this second load?"

"Sure. That would be really nice." Mandy was shocked to the tip of her boots. No one had ever paid her much mind before, particularly when it came to her needs. She hurried inside to the ladies' room while the yard guys got them loaded.

Feeling refreshed and ready to tackle the next trailer full of Mr. Shelton's new cows, she climbed up into the pickup truck and was smacked with the smell of food. It was all she could do not to weep with joy. Employees could eat at the fast-food joint at the sale barn for a discount, but she was saving every penny she could. She only spent money on one meal a day, stretching it to last and to keep the hunger at bay. The worry of being able to afford baby food and diapers never left her mind.

Phin stood on the ground with the passenger side door open. "I hope you like cheeseburgers and fries. Got you a large soda too, before I realized you may not want to drink that much." He stared at her and then burst out with a laugh that was warm and deep. She liked the sound. In spite of herself, his teasing made her giggle too.

"Why don't you let me drive, so you can eat?"

The first thought was that Calvin would have her hide if she allowed a customer to drive the company truck and then do her job, a service they provided. But then she didn't care. She hadn't eaten since mid-afternoon yesterday.

"That would be nice of you, but what about your

lunch?"

"I'm used to eating on the road. It's not a problem."

Mandy climbed down and walked around the rig, noticing that the load-out crew had turned their attention to the next lot number and were riding away from the chute. She heaved herself up again inside the cab, and they were off. Maybe no one noticed the new driver.

It was all she could do to not stuff the entire burger in her mouth. Focusing on taking small bites and chewing after each one, the mustard, broiled meat, lettuce, and tomato all came together in her mouth and made her sigh. She felt her cheeks grow warm.

"Tastes good, huh?" he asked as he gripped the steering wheel with one hand and held his lunch with the other.

"Delicious. Our cook makes one of the best burgers in the county." She cast a shy glance his way. "Thank you."

"You are very welcome."

"Do you have any kids?" Mandy asked before taking another bite.

"No. Not married."

Not much of a talker either, she noted. She hated to pry, but she felt too self-conscious stuffing her face while he drove. But then she realized the silence was comforting. It felt nice spending time with another human being, and since he knew her situation and had practically seen everything she had to flash, there was nothing to hide. There was no pressure about worrying she might slip up and say the wrong thing.

"If you need to stop, let me know," he said.

"I will."

And then he began to talk. He told her about his Angus cows, his field of dry land wheat, the chickens that his mother had named, the rooster that always attacked him, and his favorite ranch horse that turned up lame last week. He shared a bit of his faith. Obviously he was a kind and generous man who loved his family and believed in God. Mandy chewed and listened. His voice was firm and friendly, and he talked as though he had known her all his life. The time flew by, and she couldn't believe they were already at their destination.

Before long, they had unloaded the trailer at his corral. He pointed towards a thick stand of trees which shielded a clump of buildings. "That's our headquarters over there." He didn't offer to show her the house.

Phin stepped up to the sale barn's truck and tipped his ball cap to her. She rolled down the driver's side window. "I was wondering if I might call on you sometime. Maybe we could eat lunch together again."

That surprised her and made her frown. She had been honest with him to this point, so why lead him on now? "I enjoyed our conversation, Mr. Shelton, and I wish you all the best with your cows. But my mama says that I'm going to hell. You should stay as far away from me as you can. Have a nice day."

She gave him a sunny smile and didn't look back. There was still much she had to do before the workday was over and she had a long drive back to the auction barn. She imagined him standing by his pickup truck, watching the dust that hung in the air as she drove away. He would never talk to her again, probably never even notice her the next time he came to a livestock auction. And that is how she liked it. No ties, no friends, no one to ask questions.

Chapter Four

Carli

Carli watched Lank at the stove, her grandmother's bib apron tied around his waist. No shirt, camo pajama pants. He was cooking her breakfast. Probably the most perfect sight standing in her kitchen she had ever seen in her life. Her cheeks warmed when he looked at her and grinned.

"Are you ready for this, my dearest wife?"

Her heart couldn't help but flutter when he said that word. Good grief, she needed to start acting her age instead of like a teenager mooning over her first crush.

"Happy Thanksgiving," he said as he set a plate covered in steaming eggs and bacon. "Want some waffles? Just a sec."

"Our first holiday as a married couple. Definitely waffles are in order," she said as she grabbed the butter, knife poised in her hand.

"They're not homemade like Mom's, but frozen ones are good too."

"Yes, they are." Carli nodded in agreement.

He carefully lifted the cookie sheet from the

oven and slid two onto her plate. A pat of butter melted fast, and she covered that with syrup. Lank pulled the barstool closer to hers. "I love you, ya know," she said.

He leaned in for a quick kiss. "Love you too."

They ate in silence for a few moments. They must've slept past their regular breakfast time because she was extra hungry. And this tasted so good.

They needed to talk. Carli hated to break this perfect moment by bringing up the subject of an ex-girlfriend, but she couldn't get Mandy out of her head. There was no denying the way she had looked at Lank. Of course, most men are oblivious to the signals girls send. And it wasn't that she distrusted Lank. He would never do anything to hurt her or their marriage. Of that she was certain.

If she didn't say something now, she'd bust. The worry inside her would build and build, and one of the things they had agreed upon was they'd never let the sun set on their anger. More than one person had given them that advice as newlyweds.

The auction had been two days ago, and she'd already broken that promise. It wasn't that she was angry exactly; it was just a bubbling concern that burned deep in her belly and never went away. The way the girl had never taken her eyes off Lank made Carli believe there was something going on in the mind of that Miss Mandy, and whatever it was involved her husband.

Carli got the coffee pot and refilled their mugs. "I need to ask you about something."

He blew on the liquid before taking a sip. "Shoot."

"What do you know about Mandy's situation?"

"Mandy?" He looked up from his plate in surprise.

"Yes. The girl from the auction barn."

"Why do you want to know about her?"

"She looked so sad and very pregnant. Angie mentioned y'all used to date."

"Yes, we did."

"Why did you break up?"

Lank paused a minute and stuffed his mouth with a waffle. As he chewed, he avoided her gaze. "I don't remember."

"Lank!" She shot him an annoyed glance.

"Really. I seriously don't know. One minute we were going out and then the next we just went our separate ways. It wasn't like we had some deep discussion about it. That was the first time I had seen her in a long time."

"Actually, since the Rafter O party right after I first moved here and that was only a year ago. As I recall you were very happy to see her then. Did you know she was pregnant? Do you know the father?"

"It was a shock to see her like that, for sure," he said. "Colton says it was one of the older cowboys at the sale barn who is married with two kids. He moved his family away when Mandy came up pregnant."

"I hope she has family who can help her." Carli would never forget the look of utter desperation on the girl's face as they drove away from the auction that day. She finished her breakfast, relieved that he did not seem the slightest bit bothered by seeing his ex. Carli did feel relieved.

"I am seriously a good cook." He smacked his lips.

"Yes, you are. What shall we do today?"

"Whatever we want," he replied.

"I kinda wish Buck and Lola were here, but I'm

glad they are visiting their niece. I like that it's just us though."

"And my sister Kelly and her husband always visit his family in Houston for Thanksgiving. I like that it's just us, too. Have you started the turkey?"

"I thought you were cooking the turkey." She wrinkled her forehead. "This is an equal opportunity marriage. Our first tradition as man and wife can be that you cook the Thanksgiving meal. I'll go tend to the livestock." She slid off her stool and headed down the hallway.

"Not so fast. I think you forgot to buy groceries. There's nothing to cook."

"Really?" She went to the pantry to take inventory. "Here are a few cans of chicken. What do you think? Chicken instead of turkey? We could lump it together, form it into a turkey." She chuckled.

Lank wrinkled his nose. "No way."

She looked back in the pantry. "Hey, here's some Ramen noodles, soy sauce, and I've got some veggies we can cut up."

He looked at her like she had three heads.

"Think outside the box, Cowboy! We could start our own non-traditional Thanksgiving holiday tradition. A Chinese food dinner!"

"You're crazy. You know that, right?"

"I'm just being creative, Lank."

"I've got some better ideas for something that can be our new Thanksgiving tradition, Mrs. Torres."

Carli giggled and gave him a kiss. "Like what?"

"First, we make a round and break ice for the cows. Then we bring some alfalfa from the hay barn for the horses. Then we'll be cold. Snuggling in front of the fire might be nice next. It's way too cold out there to go to town for food." Lank put an arm around her shoulders.

"Well, Mr. Torres, I guess we're going to have to snuggle for the rest of the day. We've got to stay warm. Later I can make us tomato soup and grilled cheese sandwiches."

"This is sure gonna be a really different kind of Thanksgiving, but I like the way you think."

"It'll be our Thanksgiving. And we certainly have so much to be thankful for, husband." She loved saying that word. With a happy sigh Carli padded to the entry hall and shoved her feet into fur-lined boots. Lank wasn't far behind.

Chapter Five

Carli

Carli sat at a round table in the Wild Cow Ranch cookhouse staring at the faces of her employees. Lank, her husband, and Buck and Lola Wallace. Buck worked as the ranch foreman, and Lola was the cook and housekeeper, but they were more than ranch hands. They were family.

"The third Saturday in December is the date, and I want this event to be bigger and better than anything the townspeople of Dixon have ever seen." Of all the ranch projects she had participated in since becoming the new owner, Carli felt the biggest responsibility for this one. She imagined her grandparents looking down upon her with love and pride. She really wanted to do a good job for them and the whole town.

"First thing is lights," said Lola. "Tons of lights. That's how your grandparents did it every year and we all spent many, many hours on illumination detail."

"I want this place glowing like an airport runway," said Carli. "We can do this bigger and better than ever before."

Buck lowered his head and didn't look Carli in the eye. "I doubt any of those strands in storage will work after this long."

"We need to buy new then. Cattle prices were good this fall and we can invest in a few new decorations, I think. Greenery too. Wrapped around the fences. Wreaths wherever they look best. On the front door for sure. Do we have an old wagon? Or can we get one? Or a sleigh? Wouldn't that look great out front? Full of presents. Maybe an oversized, stuffed Santa Claus driving it."

Buck's eyes lit up. "What about a manger scene? Joseph, Mary, and the baby?"

"Yes!" Carli said. "That would be so nice. Let's do it all."

A knock on the door of the cookhouse snapped everyone at the table out of their imaginings, and they turned their attention in that direction. Lank's sister Kelly and her husband Matt came through the door.

Hellos went all around, and Lank stood to give his sis a hug and shake Matt's hand. "Hey, nice surprise! What are y'all doing here? Where are the little guys?"

"My mom's got them," Matt said.

"We have coffee and banana bread. Can I get you a slice?" asked Lola.

"That would be nice, Lola. Thank you," Kelly said.

Chairs scraped on cement floor as everyone scooted around to make room. Kelly and Matt moved chairs from another table and sat down after removing their jackets.

"Did we interrupt something?" asked Kelly as

she looked at the gathering.

"No, not at all. We are planning Christmas Open House," answered Carli.

Lola set mugs and plates on the table. "Carli wants to bring it back this year. Like Ward and Jean used to do."

"Oh, I loved coming out here then." Kelly's eyes lit up. "The kids are too little to remember, but Grandma Jean's hot cocoa was to die for. Wish I had her recipe. I know there was some secret ingredient. And I never could decide which cookie to try. Snickerdoodles, fudge, sugar cookies. She had so many different varieties. The lights were on both sides of the road coming into headquarters. People from Dixon lined up to drive through every evening. There were traffic jams and cars lined up to drive through headquarters!"

Carli felt a sudden sting to her heart. What she wouldn't give to have known her grandmother and been a part of a Wild Cow Christmas. Most of her life was filled with lonely times since her guardians were older and then passed away. So, Christmas ended up being just another day for her. As a new Christian though, she looked forward to celebrating, and learning and strengthening her faith, plus doing something special for the people of Dixon. She owed them that after the super barbecue they had thrown for her and Lank's engagement, and then the beautiful wedding reception. Everything had been over the top for their wedding, more than she could have ever imagined.

"So, what's going on with y'all?" Lank asked his sister.

His question turned Carli's attention to Kelly

and Matt who appeared somewhat uncomfortable and edgy. She watched them, but decided to open up the discussion, since Kelly was quiet, taking her time to answer Lank.

"We are so glad to see you both. There wasn't much time to talk at the wedding reception. How's the job going, Matt?" Carli asked.

"Funny you should bring that up. We have a huge favor to ask," said Kelly as Matt stuffed a piece of bread into his mouth; maybe his timing was on purpose. "It has to do with Matt's job."

"Are you moving?" asked Lank.

"Hope it's a big promotion," added Lola.

"Actually, it might lead to a promotion." Kelly glanced at Matt and cleared her throat.

Matt took a few gulps of coffee and looked at Lank then at Carli. "I've been invited to Europe to do a few presentations on a piece of software my team developed. It's a really cool application actually. It can—"

Kelly interrupted, "I'd like to go with him, and we were wondering if you would consider keeping the boys while we're gone."

"We should be back around Christmas," Matt said.

"Probably in time to make it to the Open House," Kelly added.

Lank couldn't hide his excitement while the smile on Carli's face froze. Over one month with two rambunctious boys in addition to everything else she had to do?

"We'll help," said Lola. "It'll be fun having kids around."

"There's always chores to keep them busy," offered Buck. "They won't be bored, that's for sure."

"When do you leave?" asked Lank.

"In two days," said Kelly. "Thank goodness we've both had to travel for our jobs, so our passports are current. We just have to figure out how to pack everything we'll need, and then we're on our way. We fly into London first."

Carli was dumbstruck. She just stared.

"My mother will help too," Matt said. "She's keeping the boys now, but she's unable to keep them for long periods of time. They just wear her out. Besides, she is leaving on a cruise in a few weeks. But, if you have anything come up and you need her, she said to be sure and call."

"We can't thank y'all enough." Kelly sighed as though a weight had been lifted from her shoulders. She touched her brother's arm.

"Happy to do it," said Lank. "That's what family does. It's going to fun, ain't it, babe?"

The smile on Carli's face hadn't moved because the words "two days" kept going around and around in her brain. Two days! She couldn't find any words to reply, so she just nodded her head like a robot. She had no idea how to take care of children, but the excitement on Lank's face made her feel guilty. Of course, he'd want to spend time with his nephews. They adored him and wanted to be cowboys, just like their uncle.

"What about school?" Carli asked.

"It's all been taken care of. They are still on Thanksgiving break, and we've made arrangements for both boys to get their assignments online during the few weeks before Christmas break. We didn't want you to worry about driving them to school, and since we'll be out of the country, they allowed us this special request."

"School stuff. That's Carli's department." Lank pointed at her.

"I can manage online work, I guess," said Carli.

"You are a godsend." Kelly stood and gave Carli a hug. "This is really important, and I'm excited to be able to support Matt. I'll email and keep in touch when I can." Then she squeezed Carli's arms, squealed, and said, "We're going to London!"

Chapter Six

Carli

Carli tidied the guest room one more time, and
then hustled to the barn. Angie should be here any
minute with that horse she had accidently bought
at the auction. An overcast gray sky matched her
mood. Leafless cottonwood trees towered along
the creek, and the brown grass crunched under her
boots as she walked. Their dog Lily Jane ran ahead,
sniffing the ground in zig zag patterns.

Lank had left early to check mineral and salt
blocks. The silence of the peaceful morning would
not reign very much longer. Lank's two nephews
would arrive soon, and while she got them settled,
Lank would be taking his sister and brother-in-
law to the airport.

God had really thrown a kink into her plans.
She had every step planned for what they needed
to do to make the Open House a success, and two
little boys would throw her entire world off track.
Lank was so excited about his nephews staying
with them, and she didn't have the heart to mention her anxiety. She would have to figure it out as

they went along.

Kelly and Matt planned to be gone several weeks but said it could stretch into a month as they were taking some extra time to celebrate their anniversary and sightsee a little. Carli said a quick prayer that she could keep two lively boys occupied that long. And keep her sanity.

A white super-cab pickup truck pulling a matching trailer ba-dumped across the cattle guard and crept through headquarters towards the corral. *Rafter O Est. 1895* and the Olsen family brand printed on the truck glinted sparkly gold in the early morning light. Angie pulled to a stop and Carli opened the door for her.

"How is he?" Carli asked, as she stepped aside so Angie could get out of her truck.

A frown covered her friend's face. "Oh, he's something, I can tell you that."

"What do you mean?" Carli followed Angie around to the back of the trailer.

"He did not want to get into the trailer, but I refused to let him win," Angie said with a look of satisfaction and a crisp nod. "We had a bit of a tussle, but I don't think he got scraped up. You never know when you get a horse at an auction what their background is. Maybe he's not been on a trailer much. But he'll learn."

"He might not do at all if he's a handful," said Carli. "I can't imagine he will be gentle enough for the riding school kids."

"He'll come around with some training. Remember, I'm donating him. But he looks underweight, so we've got to work on that first. Maybe he'll calm down with a full belly."

"Yes, he does look a little skinny." Carli nodded in agreement as she ran her hand down his neck. The horse jerked his face away and stomped one front hoof with impatience.

"I washed him. I think he might be a Dun in color, but Quarter Horse."

His coat glowed almost golden in places and his legs, tail, and mane were all black.

"That bath must've been a bit of a battle. He is beautiful and has soft eyes, but wonder why the bad attitude? It's not normal for Quarter Horses usually. And if he's twelve, shouldn't he be more mature, laid back?" Carli studied him and the horse eyed her. "We just need to work with him, that's all," Angie said. "Oh, I mean *you* need to work with him. My Dad has a whole list of jobs lined out for me, so I just don't have the time. I'm sorry."

"With some love and good food, I hope he comes around. I need him for the school. He is nice looking. Look at that dorsal stripe down his back. Does that mean he's a descendant from the Conquistador horses?"

Angie said, "I think those are called Spanish Barbs. But they may have mixed with American Quarter Horses."

"Do you know his name?"

"The papers say Peppy's Chance. There was a famous Quarter Horse named Mr. San Peppy. A cuttin' horse, I think. Maybe this one is related somehow. Hard to track those things down. For whatever reason, he didn't work out with the previous owner, so they took him to the auction."

"Let's get him into a pen. I hope he plays well with others," Carli muttered, more as wishful thinking and a silent prayer than a comment to Angie.

About the time they had the water trough filled and a few oats in the feed bucket, wheels crunched the gravel, and Carli looked up to see Matt and Kelly's SUV. They parked and got out, Matt walking around to the trunk to remove their luggage.

Lank was going to drive them to the airport while Carli watched the boys. She texted.

YOUR SIS IS HERE.

Instead of a return text, her phone rang immediately.

"Babe, I'm stuck up to my wheel hubs. You'll have to take them to the airport. Be sure to get their car and house keys, so we can take the car back and park it in their garage when we have time."

"Okay," she said. "See you soon."

"Thanks again," said Kelly. "We really appreciate this. Was that Lank? What's he got into now? It's always something with him."

"He says that he's stuck in the mud."

From the backseat spilled two boys, the youngest Zane, full of himself and not missing the new resident of the Wild Cow.

"Who's that horse?" He jetted towards the corral.

"Watch it, fella. He's not that friendly yet," warned Angie.

A mixture of the African American looks from their father and the Hispanic heritage of their mother, they were handsome boys with light brown eyes and dark, curly hair. The oldest at eight, Zachary Matthew was named after his father, and called Matt Junior. If he didn't run for public office one day, Carli would be shocked. Always a smile, always in the middle of whatever was going on with a big personality you couldn't ignore. But also reserved and business-like at times, like his dad.

"What's his name?" Zane asked. Carli remembered when she had last seen him that he was the one with all the questions and lots of "whys".

"We haven't named him yet. Maybe you boys can help me with that later." Carli turned to Matt. "Have you met our neighbor, Angie, with the Rafter O?"

Carli made the introductions. Hellos were exchanged, but Carli could tell that Matt and Kelly were anxious to leave.

"Lank is stuck in mud. Looks like I'm your ride to the airport," she said. "We could take your car, and then we wouldn't have to unload all the luggage."

"Great idea, Carli." Matt shut the trunk and got in behind the wheel. "Let's go then. Boys, get back in the car."

With protests and frowns the boys scrambled into the backseat. Carli turned to wave to Angie. "I'll talk to you later. Thanks for your donation." She laughed.

"Yep. I'll be over to help you with him as much as I can. I'm not going to abandon you."

"That's a relief." Carli waved and hopped into the back of the car with her nephews, the door barely closing before Matt had wheels rolling.

"We should be back well before Christmas." Kelly turned to look at Carli from the front seat. "And our dog is at the kennel. He loves that place. We actually bought him as a puppy from the owner, so she enjoys having him back for a visit."

One thing off her list, their dog, and then Carli felt guilty for thinking she didn't want to deal with an added pet.

As Matt pulled onto the interstate towards the Amarillo International Airport Kelly rambled over their trip, listing the European cities and sights they would be visiting. Her voice filled with excitement.

"I emailed you our itinerary," she said.

Carli barely listened, instead running through her mind the list of things she needed to get done before the Open House. If the information was in an email, she would read it later.

Matt pulled into short-term parking, and they all piled out. Carli offered to help with the luggage.

"We want to go with you," said the youngest, as tears suddenly ran down his cheeks and he tightly wrapped his little arms around his mother.

"It's okay, buddy." Kelly looked at Carli. "This is our sensitive one. Zane, listen to me. I will email when I can, and we will be back in a few weeks. You have fun at the ranch, okay?"

She hugged him close and told him she would bring back something really special for him. That appeased his tears for now, but Carli anticipated another episode around bedtime. Maybe the boys would find Lank more comforting.

The check-in line wound around, with people and rolling luggage. Carli helped Kelly and Matt get their stuff to the back of the line.

"There's no need for you and the boys to hang around," said Matt as he gave Carli a quick hug.

"Y'all go on," said Kelly. "Give me big kisses."

The boys hugged and kissed their parents, the littlest clinging to his mother for a few extra seconds before she peeled him away. "Go with Carli. You boys be good and behave. I'll be emailing and calling when I can."

"Don't worry. We will have loads of fun. And y'all have a safe journey," said Carli, and with that she spun on her heels towards the entrance, taking a small hand in each of hers. "Let's go, boys. We have a few stops to make before we head back to the ranch."

"Can we have a Whataburger?"

"It's not lunchtime yet," said the oldest with a glare to Zane.

"Would your mother let you have a cheeseburger at nine o'clock in the morning?" asked Carli.

"No," was the sullen reply followed by downcast eyes.

"Then I'm not allowing it either," said Carli. "Get in. Let's go."

Minor protests, but then she decided they could make a stop for food before heading back. Her heart went out to them, thinking of the long days and nights ahead without their parents. This was going to be tough on everybody. She understood how it felt to be alone and abandoned.

Chapter Seven

Carli

Carli pulled into the hobby and craft super store. Buck had been right about the boxes of lights in her basement. They were all outdated and she doubted she would be able to find replacement bulbs. She wasn't sure how many she needed, but more than one person had told her the barbed wire fences had been lit up on both sides of the road and all around the headquarters. It must have been beautiful when her grandparents held the event.

"Let's go, boys," Carli said, as she opened the back doors. Matt Junior climbed out, but Zane climbed over the back of his seat, pushed the latch, and hopped out of from under the rear hatch. Carli rolled her eyes and waited for him to push a button to close it before she locked the vehicle.

"Stay with me," she said. "No wandering off."

"Why are we stopping here?" Zane asked.

"Christmas lights, and we need a ton of them," she explained. "You can help me decorate when we get back."

Inside the store she grabbed a buggy, and Zane

climbed in. When she gave him a questioning look, he said, "Mom always lets me ride."

"When you were a baby," Matt Junior corrected. "He can't ride in there now. He's too big."

Carli ignored his protests. Matt Junior ran on ahead and disappeared down an aisle. So much for staying together. Christmas tunes played overhead as she made her way through rows and rows of holiday decorations to the lighting section. The shelves were bare.

"Excuse me," she asked an employee wearing a bright red vest. "Where are your Christmas lights?"

"Sold out, ma'am. That's all we have left." He pointed to a bottom shelf where a few boxes of strands of pink and one strand of lime green were arranged haphazardly. No Christmas red or multicolored.

"Thank you," said Carli as she put them in her basket. "This is better than nothing I guess." Pink for Christmas would just have to do.

On the way to the checkout register, they stopped to watch the automated holiday figures. A fat-bellied Santa dancing, a penguin singing a garbled version of *Have A Holly Jolly Christmas*, and her favorite, a group of carolers dressed in regency English garb.

"Let's get one," said Matt Junior.

"The penguin!" yelled Zane as he stood up in the buggy.

"Get down, Zane. It's dangerous. No standing. Your mother told me to keep you guys safe. And besides, you need to get out now so that I can fit these boxes in."

He complied but didn't look too happy about it. And Carli was finding out that most kids had a short attention span. One minute Zane appeared to be having the worst time of his short life, and the next he was filled with incredible joy. She started wondering about nutrition and what people said about giving kids too much sugar. She'd have to watch that.

"Look at that one!" the little guy squealed. "It's Frosty. Can we get him too?"

Carli pressed a finger to her temple and was hoping a headache was not forming. "No, Zane. I'm only getting these two. Now settle down. Let's get ready to check out."

Off like a rocket, he zoomed towards the check-out counter. *That boy needs a leash.* There was no keeping up with him. Maybe she could enlist the help of the older boy. "Matt Junior, please see that your brother does not get into any trouble. I'll catch up with you in a minute. Thank you."

Carli balanced her purchases in the cart. She imagined the inflatable penguin on one side of her front porch and the carolers at the end of the driveway. They had lights and action, and no need to break the bank for batteries. They all ran on a power cord. She remembered to pick up a few extension cords too.

Out in the car she did a quick search on her phone for other places that might have lighting. By the time she had stopped at three more stores, the protests were constant.

"If you guys will go into this building center with me, I promise we'll go get Whataburger next." That worked.

"And, Zane, you've got to promise me you won't take off running. I always need to know where you are. You could get hurt."

Dutifully following her into the store, they were more than helpful finding the right aisle. All in all, Carli ended the morning with an odd assortment of lights. Not nearly enough, but lights, nevertheless. She might have to send Lank outside the area for more.

Eager faces watched as she pulled into a parking spot at the familiar orange and white striped building. What was it about Texans and their Whataburgers?

With their food balanced on a tray, Carli followed Matt Junior to the booth that he picked out. She helped the boys spread out their food.

"I want ketchup right there," Zane pointed to a particular spot on the burger wrapping. "Don't let it touch my fries."

"Aren't you going to be dipping them in the ketchup?"

"Yes, but not till I'm ready to eat."

Carli shook her head, unwrapped her burger, and took a bite. The flavors of the crispy meat patty, vegetables, and mustard tingled her tongue. This was the best burger she'd ever tasted in her life. She took another bite. Why hadn't Lank brought her here before?

The boys had grown silent as they concentrated on their food.

"This is the best burger ever," she said. "How does yours taste?"

They nodded as they chewed and made unintelligible sounds.

"I can definitely understand how this is your favorite place." She took another bite. "Where should we put the penguin?"

"Out by the road so everybody can see it," suggested Zane.

"Can we put it right under our window? That way we can look out and see it," Junior said.

"All good suggestions. We might try it in both places and then decide which we like better. Are you boys ready to go?"

Lunch over, they piled back in the car, but not without first scuffling for a seat up front with Carli. Matt Junior was quick on the draw and called, "Shotgun!" But the little brother would not give in without a fight. "I want shotgun!"

"Nobody's getting shotgun," Carli said. *Lord, I need patience, right now please.* She massaged her eyes. "Both of you get in the back. I'll be your chauffeur. Junior, help your brother buckle his booster seat."

"Will Mom be back tomorrow?" Zane asked.

"No, sweetie. She'll be gone several weeks, but you'll have fun with Uncle Lank and me."

She looked at his forlorn face in the rearview mirror. Could he look any sadder?

"We have one more stop, and then back to the ranch. I promise."

Moans came from the backseat. She drove to the far north end of Amarillo to try one more place, with no luck. She walked back to the car with frustrated steps. There had to be street stands of Christmas lights somewhere in this town. Making sure the boys had buckled their seat belts, Carli put the car in reverse and backed up. Clunk.

"You hit a basket," said Matt Junior. "Want me to move it?"

"I'm texting Mom!" declared Zane.

"No. Do not bother your mother. She's on an airplane anyway." Wasn't he too young for a phone? "Yes, Junior, would you please return it to the front of the store? Thank you."

She kept a close eye on Junior to make sure he made it back all right, and while he pushed the buggy into a row with the others, she jumped out to see the damage. Just a minor scratch in the dark blue paint. Obvious, but not too bad.

With everyone back in the car, they got on the highway.

"No more stops," she muttered. "And no Christmas lights."

Chapter Eight

Carli

"Right in here, boys. I have the bed all ready for you and I cleaned out this dresser, so you can pick whichever drawers you want." Carli carried a small suitcase in each hand, one camouflage-style, the other depicting the action figure Thor. The boys followed her with their backpacks and favorite pillows and dropped everything in the middle of the floor. They froze and stared at the bed.

"Anything wrong?" Carli asked. She had removed the pink rose bedspread that was here when she moved in and redecorated to a more western motif with a brown cover sporting barbed wire and horses. A cowhide easy chair took up one corner, and the dresser drawers were now empty. It did not have the electronics like in their own home, but they should be comfortable.

"May I have my own room?" Matt Junior asked. "I can't sleep with him." The kid was only eight, but he talked as though he were going on twenty.

"It will have to do for now, guys. I'm sorry. This house only has two bedrooms. It's a big queen-sized mattress. Isn't that enough room for the both of you?"

"Not really," replied Junior. "He kicks."

"I do not!" Zane jumped in to defend himself.

Junior crinkled his finger to beckon Carli closer to his level and whispered in her ear, "And sometimes he pees."

"What did you say?" Zane's face was turning red. "Don't tell secrets. I'm telling Mom!"

"Tonight, it'll have to work; we'll figure something else out tomorrow."

Carli walked back to the kitchen and rummaged around in the panty for tea bags only to discover she was out of her favorite peach herbal flavor.

"Hey, babe," Lank called out from the front hallway.

She peeked her head around the corner. "Did you get your pickup washed?"

"Took forever, but yeah. That mud was packed into the wheel hubs but it's clean now."

"He touched me!" a holler came from the guest room.

"Is there any way you can think of to separate those two for tonight? We need another bed because they aren't used to sleeping together. Did your sister happen to mention that? Oh, also, maybe Zane wets the bed."

"Uh oh. No, actually Kelly didn't leave much instruction this time which is odd. She usually gives me a long list. I think she was too excited about going to Europe." Lank toed off his boots at the front door.

"Drop those muddy drawers in the laundry room, please." Carli pointed towards the back door. A thump from the guest room made them both jump.

Lank held up his hands. "I'll handle it. Let me get

these dirty jeans off first."

"There's a pair of shorts on the dryer."

Despite her curiosity to see what was going on in the guest room, Carli refrained and returned to the kitchen. She sat at the bar, sipping her hot tea.

She loved this kitchen. The place where her Grandma Jean had cooked and fed her family. It was outdated now with appliances and faded colors from the 1970s. Probably top of the line in the day. Carli had thought a lot about remodeling, but she felt her grandmother's presence and didn't want to lose it. She imagined the conversations that must have gone on here. It made her feel a part of the Jameson family even though she never knew any of them. Life was so strange.

"I am going to cook you my famous dish that only I know how to make," said Lank. With a dramatic wave of a spatula, he pointed at the boys. "Your table awaits, gentlemen."

The boys climbed up on to the barstools with big smiles and twinkling eyes. Carli had discovered that Uncle Lank could be quite entertaining.

"What are we having for dinner, oh master chef?" Carli asked.

"Fried bologna sandwiches," Lank announced.

"Is that a lunch meat?" asked Junior.

"Mom says we can't have preservations," added Zane.

"Since I'm your mother's little brother, I'm allowing it this one time."

Carli realized that he must mean preservatives. Score one for the Aunt and Uncle.

"Now watch and learn. This is a great family secret, and you must not tell anyone the recipe.

Can you keep a secret?"

"Yes," they both shouted at once.

"What is the trick to this deliciousness, oh great one?" asked Carli.

"Butter," Lank said with a wink. They watched as he fried four slices of bologna and placed them between two slices of bread.

"I'd like some mustard." Carli stood to walk to the refrigerator.

"No!" should Lank. "You must not destroy the masterpiece. Take a bite now."

Carli shrugged her shoulders and bit into her sandwich. She had to admit it was delicious.

"Can we have two?" Junior asked.

They laughed and made jokes and ate.

When everyone was full, Carli hustled them to the bathroom for showers.

"Brush your teeth and find your pajamas," she called out to them as they hurried down the hall. Why is it that boys never walk anywhere? After she had the kitchen cleaned, she made another cup of tea and wondered how the boys were doing.

More thumping from the guest room. When she walked in, Lank had the boys in a headlock on the floor and all three were giggling like a gaggle of geese.

"That's enough. Bedtime," Carli said. "And both of you be sure to use the bathroom one more time."

All faces held deep disappointment, but she stood firm. This had been a long day.

Lank tucked his nephews in. "I'll be right back."

"Did you brush your teeth?" Carli asked them. Both nodded their heads.

Lank returned with a rope which he laid out on

the bed between them. "This is the magic rope. If you cross it, you break the magic. If you stay on your side, you'll have good dreams."

"Mom always listens to our prayers," said Zane with a pout.

"You're in luck tonight, buddy. Two of us to hear your prayers." Lank smiled at Carli.

At the same time, they sat up and bowed their heads. Zane went first. "Bring mommy back soon. Amen."

Matt Junior was more direct. "Dear God. I pray that father has a successful business meeting and mother gets to shop. Amen." Lank and Carli looked at each other.

"Goodnight, you two. See you in the morning." Carli pulled the cover up over Zane's small feet.

"Will we have to find more Christmas lights?"

"Can we ride a horse?"

"Can we have cereal for breakfast?"

"Do we have to take more showers while we're here?"

"Enough," said Carli, her patience wearing thin, but she couldn't help smiling at their enthusiasm. "All questions will be answered tomorrow. No more for tonight."

Lank winked, tucked the covers around them one more time. Carli turned off the light switch and went back to her tea as Lank headed to the shower. Before he disappeared into the bathroom, he turned and wrapped an arm around her shoulders.

Kissing her temple, he murmured, "Thanks for filling in for me today. Taking my sister to the airport and dealing with nephews."

"Sure," she said. "We're a team now. Whatever

you have to deal with, that means I have to deal with it too."

"After tucking my nephews in, I wonder about the nights you went to bed without anyone hearing your prayers. Is that how it was for you?"

The question caught her off guard. She had never shared much with Lank about her childhood. That was so long ago, and remembering seemed like a lonely fog that had hung over her head.

She smiled at her husband. "I have you now. That is all that matters."

Watching two little boys grow up surrounded by so much love made her wonder if Taylor Miller, her birth father, ever thought about what his life might have been like if he had known about her. If her mother, Michelle, hadn't given her up. What if Michelle had told Taylor that she was pregnant? Would he have taken on the responsibility of a family at only eighteen? No way to know that now, and since her guardians were both dead there was no way to ask them about the past either. Some questions would never be answered.

But that didn't mean she couldn't have a relationship with her birth father now. How should she approach him? He missed twenty-eight years of her life and there was no way of getting those back. She didn't even know if he wanted a relationship, although he seemed really nice at her wedding and reception. But how would his wife and kids feel about her disruption into their family?

Carli sighed and collapsed into the leather chair. She stared into the fire and sipped her tea. Maybe the past should be left where it belongs, in the past. For the present she had to figure out what to do with little boys for a month. Energetic boys. What did she even know about kids?

Chapter Nine

Dear Matt Jr., Zane, Lank, and Carli,

Well, we arrived safely in London! It was a LONG flight—almost 11-12 hours! From Amarillo the plane took about an hour to get to Dallas and stayed there for another hour. Not sure why they have to do that but anyway . . . then we flew over the Pond—that's what they call the Atlantic Ocean! What do you think of that, boys? Maybe Uncle Lank and Aunt Carli can show you on the computer what a BIG body of water that is. The good thing was we got to sleep on the plane (a little uncomfortable—not like our own bed), and then woke up in London!

I've got to go for now. The WiFi connection is not the greatest and sometimes cuts me off. And texting doesn't work. I'm going to find out if I can add international to my cell phone so I can call you. Dad knows how all of that works. We didn't have time before we left to go to the phone store.

WE LOVE YOU BOYS WITH ALL OUR HEARTS!

Please be good boys for Aunt Carli and Uncle Lank. Make Mama and Daddy proud.

Love,
Mom

Chapter Ten

Taylor

Taylor Miller had a Honey-Do list as long as his arm—wash the vehicles, rotate tires; well, those were on his list. His wife Karissa wanted him to organize the garage and help her transport a bunch of supplies she had been gathering for her sorority's service project to the women's shelter. Boxes of various items had been stored in their garage and to move them would help to free up some space. Plus, the shelter was always out of items—paper goods, linens, canned goods, some toys. Taylor was happy to do whatever she needed and had actually taken off from work for an afternoon to help. It had been an interesting few weeks; one highlight being the wedding of a daughter he never knew he had—Carli Jameson.

"Hey, darlin'," he said to Karissa. "I'd also like to take some of our extra Christmas lights over to the Wild Cow sometime. Buck said Carli wants to light up ranch headquarters like an airplane runway. They could use them for their big display, and we have extra."

"Oh, right. Carli is bringing back her grand-parents' tradition of lighting the ranch up for the townsfolk. I like that idea. When is the big day?"

"Third Saturday of December. Buck called yesterday and mentioned it."

Their daughter Shayla came down the stairs, all smiles, and only caught her dad's last comment.

"That's when my boutique is having their Christmas party," she said. "Y'all are coming, aren't you? We can bring our families. My boss is catering all kinds of food and I think the employees are getting Christmas bonuses. I sure hope so. I could use it." She sported a big grin and swung her head to toss her long hair over one shoulder. "My boss said it's a big dress up affair and everyone is going. Should be super elegant. I've got to figure out what to wear."

It was hard to interrupt Shayla. She was happy, excited, and on a roll. Taylor didn't always see his twenty-two-year-old in this good of a mood. Oftentimes, she was upset about her clothing, or the customers she had to accommodate where she worked at the fancy store, or what her friends were posting on social media.

But Taylor had to jump in. "Shayla, that's the day of Carli's big Christmas Open House for the whole town. I haven't talked to her yet, but I assume she'll want us all to be there. It'll be fun. Buck said he could use my help."

Any part of a smile immediately slid off Shayla's face. "Mom, I told you about my work Christmas party. Remember? You already said you and Dad would come."

Karissa looked at her husband, then daughter. "Shayla, I didn't know the date of your event or

Carli's either. But we'll figure this out."

Karissa filled small bowls with fruit as Taylor manned the stove, cooking bacon.

"I told you the date, Mom! Oh, sure. Now that *she's* in your life, you'll do everything she wants. What about me? I can't believe this."

"Take it easy, Shayla," Taylor said with forced authority in his voice. "Like your mom said, we'll figure things out and try to make both events if we can. I'd like to see some of my old neighbors from Dixon. I grew up there you know." It would be nice seeing some of the people he had gone to high school with. Many of his classmates had stayed to raise their families in Dixon, and he felt sure the whole town would turn out for this event. Carli was doing a good thing by bringing back the tradition.

"Shayla, why don't you sit down?" Karissa said to her daughter. "We'll make French toast if you want, and we can all talk about it."

"I don't want to talk. I know you'll decide to go to Carli's event instead of mine. Seems like ever since you found out about her that's all we hear. 'Carli this' and 'Carli that'. What about me? I'm the daughter that's been here all along."

"That's not really true, sweetie. We want to go to your party too." Karissa put a hand on her daughter's shoulder. "You know this is an adjustment for the whole family. It was a shock when your dad found out she was his daughter. We love you more than anything in the world. But there will be times when we all have to compromise a little."

Shayla's eyes grew large, full of hurt, bordering on anger. "Compromise? I have an event at work. You said you'd come. Now Carli has an event, and you say you need to be there too. Doesn't sound like a compromise to me."

Taylor spoke up as he recognized the hurt on her face. He was determined to keep his words calm. "Shayla, what time is your party? Maybe there's a way we can go to yours and then to Carli's."

Shayla rolled her eyes and exhaled a big sigh. The over-dramatic daughter who required them all to step easy around her.

Karissa, the peacemaker, said, "That's a good idea. See, honey, we can work it out. Don't worry about it now. Let me fix you some breakfast."

Shayla shook her head without a word. A tear formed in her eye and slid down her cheek. Looking at her mother she quietly said, "I'm not hungry. I'm going out with my friends." And with that she left the kitchen and hurried upstairs.

"That didn't go so well." Taylor set the bacon fork down on a small dish and looked at his wife. "What now?"

"Why don't you find out from Buck what time their event is happening? I think Shayla's is at seven."

Taylor sipped his coffee and braced himself against the counter. "I've got a bad feeling about this. The Wild Cow will probably turn on the Christmas lights right when it gets dark. That's early now, around five-thirty. Shayla's party starts at seven. Takes forty-five minutes from Amarillo to Dixon. It'll be hard to be in two places at once. Maybe we can go to Carli's first, then to Shayla's. And back to Carli's."

Karissa came over to Taylor who had taken a seat on one of the stools. She put an arm around his shoulder and stroked his hair. He leaned an elbow on the counter and held his forehead.

"Now don't start your worrying, Taylor. We *will* figure this out, sweetie. Remember, *this too shall pass.*"

"It's really important that we be there for Carli, I think. This event is important to her."

Karissa nodded her head in agreement. "I think you're right. I think it's more important than she would admit. We need to support her."

Taylor sighed; his fork froze in midair. "I don't understand how we raised a daughter than can be so self-centered at times. We disciplined her. Maybe we never denied her enough? Some days, I can't even relate to what is going on in her head."

They ate their breakfast in relative silence. Karissa attempted conversation but Taylor hardly answered, still in deep thought.

Soon he got up from the table and took his dish to the sink. "I'm not that hungry. I need to run in to the office this morning, but I'll get started in the garage right after lunch."

"Now, sweetie, please don't let Shayla get to you. Why don't you call Buck later? Or we can go over there with the extra lights. Ask him what's going on that day."

"All right, darlin'. She was such a sweet little girl. I just want her to be a kind-hearted woman." He gave her a kiss on the cheek and started for the side door to load the women's shelter boxes into his truck.

"And I think," Karissa said, "we need to let the children make their own decisions. They might surprise us and do the right thing."

Taylor turned before walking out. "I hope you're right."

Chapter Eleven

Taylor

Washed and vacuumed vehicles: Check. Rotated tires: Check. Taylor loaded boxes for the women's shelter into his truck and rearranged the garage. Looked pretty good. Would have been nice to have had his son Hud's help but he was working. Hard to tie that boy down anyway.

Sweaty and nearly worn out, Taylor went to the kitchen for some sweet tea. His wife, Karissa, was seated in a small alcove at the end of the counter typing on the computer.

"Hey, sweetie, how's it going?"

Taylor pulled a paper towel off the roll and swiped his face and neck. "I'm done. Gonna take a quick shower. You ready to drop the boxes at the shelter? Then you want to come with me to the Wild Cow?"

"Sounds like a plan." Karissa stood. "We might have extra lights in the basement storage. I'll check while you rinse the dust off. I'm ready to leave when you are."

***

Taylor pulled into the driveway of a cheery, blue Craftsman style house a couple miles outside of downtown Amarillo. Karissa had told him this was called a transitional shelter to help women get back on their feet.

"Tell me about your new project," he said.

"Some of these girls struggle with drugs, alcohol, financial, or other issues. Some need a job or childcare. Our community has some shelters in the downtown area, while other domestic violence shelters were hidden in different parts of town or outside of town. They become safe houses, to protect the women from abusive partners. They keep their locations very confidential as sometimes abusers come after their victim, again and again."

"What a nightmare for these women." Taylor studied the property and was impressed at how neat and clean it appeared.

"I called ahead. Mary should be watching for us."

Just as Karissa opened the vehicle door, a gray-haired woman met them in the driveway. "Thanks so much for bringing these supplies. We really appreciate it."

"Hi, Mary. We're happy to do it." The women had met before at a fundraising event that Karissa's sorority had sponsored. "This is my husband, Taylor."

"Nice to meet you, Taylor. Thank you so much for helping." She extended her hand and he held it.

"Anytime."

Mary opened the garage for them, and Taylor began transferring the boxes.

She said, "I'm sorry I can't show you inside the

house." She looked up at Taylor. "Some of the women get skittish around men. I hope you understand."

"Of course," he said.

Karissa and Mary exchanged a few words about another sorority fundraiser planned for the new year, then they hugged their goodbyes. Mary gave Taylor a tight squeeze too.

On the way to the Wild Cow, Taylor was quieter than usual. Karissa looked over at him and said, "Thanks for helping me get those supplies to the shelter, sweetie."

"Sure, darlin'."

"Did you like Mary?"

"Yeah. Nice lady."

"You okay?"

"Yeah. Just thinkin'."

"About what?"

"Why men do what they do."

"What men?"

"The ones who caused those women to be in that shelter. And the other shelter for women who have been hit. Then I was thinking about Carli."

"What about Carli? She was never hit."

"No. As far as I know, she wasn't. I wonder about her mother, Michelle, though. She got in with the wrong crowd. No telling what kind of nuts she was involved with."

"You're a good man, Taylor Miller. A thoughtful man." She touched his arm on the console. "And I love you very much."

***

At the Wild Cow Ranch, Taylor pulled his truck to a stop in front of Carli's house where a group of people stood. Buck, Lank, Lola, and Carli all turned to look at them. They stopped what they were doing and walked closer to the driveway.

"The gang's all here." Taylor chuckled.

Lank was picking up a box and two little boys were running around a stack of boxes.

Buck called out a greeting. "Hey, Taylor! Glad you came."

Taylor exited the truck and shook Buck's hand. "Well, I told ya I had some extra lights, so we wanted to drop them off. Do you remember my wife, Karissa?"

Greetings were exchanged all around.

"Great, thanks!" Carli said. "Let's take them over to the cookhouse."

"That's our staging area," Buck explained. "You bring your lights and I'll grab another one of the boxes."

"Puttin' me to work already, are you?"

The two men laughed and made their way to the cookhouse. Taylor turned and winked at Karissa who was in capable hands with the ladies.

***

Carli was surprised and happy at the sight of her father's truck pulling to a stop in her driveway. She followed Lola over to say hello to Karissa.

"How are you doing?" she asked.

Carli smiled but turned to wrangle Zane and Junior, who were playing shoot 'em up cowboys around the tower of boxes. "You'd better not knock those down, boys. There are fragile ornaments inside."

Suddenly her dog Lily Jane appeared, and Zane chased her.

"Do *not* scare her, Zane." Carli's jaw tightened and she pursed her lips in an effort not to yell in front of their guests. She lost the battle. "Stop it, guys! Now why don't you boys go on over to the cookhouse and catch up with your Uncle Lank? Go straight there. And be nice to Lily Jane."

Lola leaned closer to Karissa. "We started this the other day, but we keep finding more decorations. The guys brought some boxes up from the cookhouse storage and then neighbors donated more. It's a little chaotic here." She smiled.

"Who are the little boys?" Karissa asked.

"Oh, those are Lank's nephews. His sister and her husband are out of the country so Lank and Carli are taking care of the boys. They're full of energy, to say the least." Lola shrugged.

"Aren't they always? Boys, I mean."

"Hi, Karissa." Carli came over, breathless and her face feeling flushed. "Sorry for the noise and craziness."

"Gosh, no bother. I've got a grown one of those, but I remember when Hud was a wild child. Always full of energy."

"Where are they now?" Lola asked.

"I asked Lank to keep his eye on them. The boys are going to hang out with the men for a while." Carli slumped in one of the chairs on the front porch. "Whew. They sure run me ragged. Have a seat, ladies."

"I can get us some tea," Lola said.

"That would be nice, thanks. You want to check in my house for tea?"

"I'll just go to the cookhouse. I've got some ready. It's no trouble."

"Why don't we just follow you there instead?" Carli asked. "That way you won't have to carry anything back here."

"You'll run into the little rascals," Lola said. "Might be more chaos over there."

"Oh, well, I guess there's no hiding from them forever." Carli and the ladies all chuckled.

As they walked, Karissa said, "Hey, ladies, we've got a problem maybe you can help us with."

"Sure, what is it?" Lola said.

"I think Taylor might ask Buck the same thing, but I thought I'd bring it up to you." Karissa smiled.

"What's the problem?" Lola asked.

"It's Shayla. She's upset because the boutique where she works is having their Christmas party the same night you're having the Open House. Of course, she wants us to go to her work party. Her boss invited all of the employees' families. But Taylor wants to help Buck and Carli with the Open House. He also wants to go to Shayla's party. We don't know how we can be in two places at once."

"What time is Shayla's party?" Lola asked.

"Seven o'clock," Karissa said.

Carli didn't make eye contact, but said, "You should go to Shayla's party."

"Maybe you could come here first," Lola said. "When does it get dark? Around five-thirty or so now?"

Karissa and Carli nodded their heads.

Lola was all upbeat as usual. "So come here

first, stay a while, Christmas lights go on around five-thirty, and by six-fifteen head to Shayla's boutique. It'll be pushin' it but it'll work."

Karissa looked relieved. "I was thinking the same thing. Gee, what we do for our kids."

"If you ladies will excuse me, I'll start the coffee pot." Lola disappeared into the kitchen.

Karissa smiled and laughed, then looked at Carli. There was an awkward silence. "I didn't mean that in a strange way. Taylor wants to help you also. He hopes you both can get to know one another better. In fact, why don't you and Lank come over for dinner soon?"

Carli had wanted a family, a real family, her whole life. Now that she knew who her birth father was, the possibility of family was becoming real. But why did it feel so darned awkward?

She swallowed and answered Karissa, her voice cracking. "I'll mention it to Lank. Thank you for the invite."

Chapter Twelve

Mandy

"Mandy? You're here early."

She woke with a start at the sound of her name but couldn't roll off the makeshift cot quick enough before her boss, Calvin, walked into the storeroom.

"What are you doing?"

Still exhausted, she blinked and tried to clear the fuzz from her brain. Her stomach growled and his questions kept coming.

He lowered his head and studied the room. His eyes widened in surprise. "Are you sleeping here every night?"

"It's just temporary." She stood, planted a smile on her face, and adjusted her shirt back over her protruding belly. The same shirt she had worn all day yesterday. Thank goodness exhaustion had won last night and she hadn't taken the time to change into a gown that was as big as a boat sail.

"What's wrong with your apartment?" he asked.

Only the fact she had been tossed out on her ear, not to mention the lousy landlord had kept her television, laptop, and DVD player. Enough electronics and used furniture to more than put towards two months' back rent and then some. Everything she owned was now in her car.

"It's being remodeled." Lame, but it was the first thing that came to mind. The frown on Calvin's face eased. He seemed to buy it.

"I guess it's okay, but where are you taking a shower?"

"At the truck stop on the interstate. I usually go early in the morning and eat breakfast there too, but I overslept."

"This is only temporary, right?"

"Yes, sir. Thank you, Calvin. I really appreciate it."

"I need you to tally up those tickets from Tuesday and make out a bank deposit. The numbers are short. See if you can find the error, will you?"

"Sure."

If he'd ever disappear into his office for one minute, she could grab her toothbrush and slip into the restroom. She had no idea if she had any clean shirts left. Every penny she made went into her bank account in anticipation of being able to afford diapers. A quick check of all the vending machines around town usually turned up enough spare change to wash a load of laundry, but they had been so busy lately at the sale barn. It was all she could do to make it to the cot and collapse after everyone else had left for the day.

Tonight, she would have to take time to sort through the pile of clothes in the backseat of her car. She could wash out a few pairs of underwear and tops in the utility room sink and they'd be dry by morning.

She waddled out into the hall and looked both

ways for her boss. After freshening up in the restroom, Mandy filled the coffee pot and switched it on, and then wandered into the sale arena to pick up trash and stretch her legs before she sat down at the computer. She walked back and forth between the rows, stuffing garbage into a plastic trash bag. Breathless from stooping, she leaned against a chair back.

Her eyes darted to the auctioneer's desk that rose behind the fenced show ring. Sometimes on sale days she could swear he was standing there, his familiar straw hat, crisp white shirt, red tie, and blue sports jacket. Her pulse always raced, and then the image was gone like a puff of smoke leaving her shriveled and weak.

His face would be forever implanted in her mind with full clarity since the first time she laid eyes on him. Jeff was the most beautiful thing she had ever seen in her life. Ten years older, educated, charming, and he had noticed her from the very first day he started the new job. She had been drawn to him immediately.

Mandy took the steps into the booth slowly and deliberately, one at a time as she heaved her bulk upwards. Stooping to pick up a few scraps of paper and several pencils that had rolled off the counter, she then pulled the trash bag from the can. A deep sadness washed over her.

Jeff had been the reason for the conflict with her mother. Of course, she had found out about him. You can't pluck an eyebrow in a small town without someone taking note and telling what they thought they knew. And of course, her mother's church friends had reported that he was married.

Lerlene Milam went ballistic, and even said a curse word which had never come out of her mouth before. They both said horrible things to each other, but there wasn't anything Mandy could do about it by then. She was hopelessly and helplessly in love. She wouldn't listen to her mother, and she didn't want to hear what anybody had to say about Jeff. He promised her the world. They planned their future and she never looked back.

When he began controlling her more and more, she'd ignored it. One of his rules was that she had to drive straight home, and sometimes he followed to make sure of it. Seeing her friends was out of the question; he was all she needed in her life. He didn't want her to enroll in the community college. With a knack for numbers, her mother encouraged her to get an accounting certificate. But Jeff had said no. She obeyed and soon fell in line with the terms of their relationship. There had been many red flags now that she thought back, but she had trusted him. With her heart. With her life. She loved him. And he blamed her for getting pregnant.

Blinded in her fantasy, she never saw it coming. The day she came to work, and he didn't. That was that. Poof. He was gone. But had left a reminder. And she couldn't help but love that too.

"Mandy!"

With the tail end of her shirt, she wiped the moisture from her cheeks. "Up here," she called out. "I'm on my way." Her stomach growled again. Hopefully somebody thought to bring doughnuts, and the coffee should be done by now in the break room.

"Let's get you some breakfast, my little man." She patted her big belly and waddled towards her office.

Chapter Thirteen

Carli

"When can you help me with Open House stuff?" Carli watched Lank pull on his boots.

"I need to cake three pastures, a mill is down in P2, and then if there's any daylight left, I'll hang a few Christmas lights."

She raised her eyebrows and crossed her arms.

"I promise," he said, leaving a warm kiss on her cheek.

"I'm going to sort through the basement some more to see what I can find. Have a good morning." Carli stepped out on the front porch to watch her husband climb into his pickup truck. If they didn't get started on decorations soon, they'd barely make the Open House date and then it would be time to take it all down. Pulling her sweater closer, she paused to admire the rising sun shoot streaks of orange and yellow through gray clouds.

Zane suddenly appeared at her side. "I'm hungry."

"Well then, let's find you some breakfast."

They turned and went to the kitchen where she pulled out four boxes of cereal from the pantry. He studied the different brands and looked at her.

"Mom makes me oatmeal," he said.

"I am completely out of oatmeal, but I will start a grocery list. You can have it tomorrow morning."

"Is my mom coming home today?" A deep frown creased his forehead and he slumped in the chair.

"Matt Junior! Hurry up. We need to get online and check your assignments." Carli's phone tingled. "My phone just reminded me."

Junior appeared and glanced at the cereal boxes. "I don't like any of those." He crossed his hands on the table and looked at her with big, sad eyes.

"Eggs? Bacon? Peanut butter sandwich?" Wait. She had no fresh bread. Each option was met with a shake of the head. No.

"Can I call my mom?" The littlest had a stubborn streak like his uncle.

Carli sat down and crossed her arms on the table too, defeated and lost for ideas of what to do next.

"I'm hungry," announced Junior.

Carli simply pointed to the boxes of cereal. He responded with a wrinkle of his nose.

"Okay. Get your clothes on. We're going to town for breakfast."

Carli turned back to her room to change. Surely Belinda at the B&R Beanery and Buns had something for two hungry boys. After all, buns was part of the business name. If not, Carli would let them pick the cereal at the grocery. It wasn't even nine o'clock and the nephews had already won a round. It was going to be a long day.

On the way to town, Carli made a grocery list in her mind. There wasn't any noise coming from the backseat to distract her. They must be too hungry and still sleepy. She had no idea what growing boys liked to eat. Thank goodness for Lola and her ability to cook meals. How she came up with so many different ideas for dishes amazed Carli. One thing for sure, she was not going to give in and let them pick out a lot of junk food.

Carli pulled into a parking place at the front door of the B & R Beanery in Dixon, and both boys unbuckled their seatbelts and flew before the wheels had completely stopped rolling. She started to holler but it was too late. Instead, she hopped out and followed them inside. She'd chastise them later.

The bell tinkled as Carli pushed the door open. She always paused to focus on the aroma of coffee beans and the slight hint of baked pastry. Belinda and her husband Russell had perfected their roasting process, and Belinda was a superb baker. This coffee shop was the one place where Carli could relax, and oftentimes find a sympathetic ear and a friend who wasn't afraid to tell her what she needed to hear.

"You've got some hungry boys." Belinda greeted her with a laugh. "I've got bananas and fresh blueberry muffins, and two cups of chocolate milk coming right up."

Both boys stared at Belinda with eager faces over the top of the front counter. They could barely tear their eyes away from the raised platter of muffins, as Belinda lifted the lid and placed two on napkins.

"My mother is in Europe," announced Zane.

"Aunt Carli is doing a fine job then, if she brought you here for breakfast. Best place in town." Belinda sent Carli a questioning glance.

"The usual for me, please." And then looking

at the boys, she said, "Let's sit here." Carli pulled out chairs for them at a back table where she and Belinda always sat.

"Yes, they are staying with us. It's cold and windy. Any ideas on how to keep two energetic boys entertained indoors?"

"Let me think on that."

"What is that?" Matt Junior asked, pointing at the shiny metal contraption that filled one corner of the coffee shop. Of course, young boys would be drawn to it with the mysterious gauges and knobs.

"That is where we roast our coffee beans."

Carli settled into her seat propping her legs on a chair and sipped her latte while Belinda morphed into coffee connoisseur mode and explained how the roaster worked, the industry of coffee beans, and went so far as to take the boys in the back for a guided tour of the storeroom. The uneaten bananas and muffins quickly forgotten.

"How's married life?" asked Belinda as she returned to the table while the boys dug into their food.

"It's wonderful, but my life really hasn't changed much. We are right back to ranch work since we didn't go on a honeymoon."

"Why didn't you go anywhere?" Belinda wiped the table of something only she saw, then returned the ever-present rag to her apron.

"After numerous discussions on the subject before and after the wedding, we couldn't agree on a place. Lank only wants to go somewhere he can wear his boots and hat, so that left the Gulf Coast out. I can't imagine him walking down the beach in his full punchy garb. I'm not really a mountain hiking type person, although I do miss the woods of Georgia. But that's too far."

"Russell and I went to Six Flags Over Texas in Arlington for our honeymoon. Usually a place for families, but we had a blast on the rides." A smile lit Belinda's face as she recalled the memory. "We acted like silly teenagers. It was BK—before kids."

"Sometimes it seems Lank and I have so little in common." Carli sighed.

"Y'all are perfect for each other. What're you talkin' about?"

"It was a whirlwind romance, that's for sure."

"My mama always said, your heart will know but ya gotta take your head with you too."

Carli nodded in agreement. She argued with her heart and her head for many months, but Lank had persisted. "When you find the right one, it's just so easy and natural."

"That is so true," agreed Belinda as she stood to wait on a customer.

"Let's load up and go to the store, guys." Carli gave her friend a wave. Reluctantly the boys followed her to the pickup truck. She backed into the street and drove one block to the grocery.

Dixon has two small supermarkets, both owned by brothers. One was modern, well lighted and well stocked while the other offered dusty items stacked haphazardly on ancient shelves. The wide plank floor squeaked under foot and the only cashier was as ancient as the building. Carli usually preferred the older, no-frills, never any kind of holiday decorations store. Jack's Grocery. Or Grumpy Jack's as he was known around town. But for today's purposes she parked in front of Roy's

Grocery. He would have more of a variety of items the boys might like.

The holiday decorations were over the top, and her nephews could not be swayed away from the towering Christmas tree. It was impressive. A variety of candy served as ornaments, and a train circled around the bottom. Carli stopped to stand between the brothers, and they all watched for several minutes.

"Wonder where that train would go, if it could," mused Junior.

"To the North Pole," answered Zane.

"Can I have apple sauce?" asked Junior, ignoring his brother's comment.

Carli smiled. Now that's a healthy treat. "Yes, you may. Find the cereal you like too."

With the boys in tow, she pushed a basket up and down the aisle as they made their choices, commenting on their likes and dislikes and making note of what their mother allowed them to eat.

They loaded the basket with all their favorites, within reason. Carli considering each purchase and felt a bit of pride that she had taken control of her two charges and had things well in hand.

"Hey, Grandma, can I have these cookies?" yelled Zane, the youngest.

His older brother punched him in the arm. "She's our aunt, dummy."

"Owww, stop it," Zane said with a punch to the gut as his reply. "I'm telling Mom that you called me a name."

"Boys. Boys." Carli hurried to pull them apart, but they were already on the floor wrestling. "Let's get our groceries and get back to the ranch."

"When we stay with our other grandma, she lets us have chocolate milk and chocolate cake." Zane turned pleading eyes to her.

"No cake, guys." Carli ignored the sad-faced frown.

"This is my favorite." Zane held up a blue box of mac and cheese and pulled several off the shelf. One hit the floor with a rattle. Carli nodded her head. "Just one box. Put the others back."

Lank's sister had given her cash for food which she had absentmindedly left at the house. Now she was glad to be at Roy's Grocery and able to use her credit cards since the other store didn't take plastic.

On the way home, Carli's mind kept wandering to Junior's question. Where would that train go if it could jump the tracks? As if he had been reading her mind, Junior asked again. "Where do you think that train would go, Aunt Carli?"

"To the mountains, I suppose," she replied. "Where do you think it wants to go?"

"To find my mom and dad and bring them back home safe, of course."

Carli did not have a reply to that. Junior was the thinking one and apparently a worrier like her. She needed to do everything she could to keep these boys occupied. Ranch work was the only solution she could come up with, but the winter made that next to impossible.

"Can we get a Whataburger?" Zane begged.

"You just ate breakfast. Sorry, Dixon doesn't have one of those. Where does all that food go that you eat? It sure is a mystery to me."

"Our mom says we're growing," said Zane.

"You got that right."

Chapter Fourteen

Carli

With breakfast out of the way and her pantry full of kid-friendly snacks, Carli was itching to get busy on the decorations. In her mind she envisioned a spectacular light show with giant snowflakes hanging from the tree limbs that would transform the Wild Cow Ranch headquarters into a winter wonderland. People would drive from miles around and talk about Jean's granddaughter who brought back the traditions of the Wild Cow Ranch. Even bigger and better.

"I'll be in the basement, guys," she said as she passed through her back study. She had sat the boys in front of her computer to watch a movie.

"Can we ride horses?" Zane asked. That boy could not sit still for one minute.

"It's a little cold out today and I don't know where your Uncle Lank is, and I need to work downstairs a minute. Maybe we can go riding tomorrow." Carli took the steep steps one-by-one and felt around for a light switch.

One corner of the dimly lighted basement bulged

with stacked boxes simply labeled DECORATIONS. She reached high and dragged down the top one, which landed with a dusty thud. Pulling off the lid, she peered inside. Red satin balls. Nothing she could use outside really. She pulled another box down, and another until she found something she could use.

"Yay!" she said out loud just before she sneezed. Giant plastic ornaments in faded colors and over-sized plastic candy canes. Perhaps they would look good hanging from the evergreen trees that stood on one side of the garage. She lugged the box up-stairs and went back downstairs for more.

What she needed was yards and yards of lights to line the barbed wire fences along both sides of the road into headquarters. She envisioned red lights outlining her porch, and maybe blue for the cookhouse.

Eventually the garage was filled with the same boxes once stacked in the basement. If only Grand-ma Jean had left instructions or at least some pictures from years past. She should look through some more photo albums, or maybe just do her own thing. One more trip downstairs revealed a corner that had not been cleaned out. Hopefully there would be hidden treasures. Removing boxes of blankets and quilts she uncovered a large cabinet that stretched from floor to ceiling, full of metal cans lining the shelves.

Carli picked one up and held it to the light, no-ticing the crude hole punches that formed uneven designs over the tin surface. Some were shaped in crosses, snowflakes, and other unrecogniz-able forms. They looked like very crude candle holders made from old, recycled tin cans. There must have been hundreds of them. Why would her grandmother need this many candle holders? Perhaps decorations for an event the ranch might have hosted at the cookhouse, or maybe they were stored here for the church.

Carli rummaged around for a few minutes more, and luckily found a jumbled clump of lights with large, old-fashioned bulbs. She hurried upstairs to plug them in and, miracle of miracles, they all burned bright red, blue, green, and white. They would work perfect for her porch.

She pressed Lank's name on her cell phone, but no answer. They could get a lot done this afternoon if she could locate Lank and Buck. She'd just put the boys to work.

"Hey, guys. I need your help. We're hanging Christmas lights on the front porch. Grab your boots, coats, and hats. It's a bit chilly this morning."

Groans and protests followed.

"Hot chocolate when we're done," she said.

"Can we go see Belinda again?" begged Zane.

"Her hot chocolate is the best," agreed Junior.

"Okay, we can run back to town if you want." She was powerless to argue with their logic. Carli shoved her woolen cap on and dragged the lights to the front porch. She came back inside to find an extension cord.

"What do we do?" Junior asked with sad eyes but willing to do anything for the promise of food and drink.

"I also have some stuff you can hang in the trees," she said. She tapped Lank's number one more time. They must be in the pasture somewhere which made her worry if maybe something was wrong with a cow or windmill. Pushing the concern from her mind, she focused on the task at hand. She had the boys help her carry the ladder and a small step stool from the kitchen. It wasn't long before they were all consumed with the Christmas spirit and a job to do.

"Can I use this?" asked Junior as he pulled the ladder in place.

"I want to climb it too," said Zane.

"One at a time on the ladder, but you can only go halfway up." Carli felt as though she was getting the hang of handling two boys. It was an impossible task to remember all the rules as they always seemed two steps ahead of her.

"That looks really great, guys." Carli stopped to admire the giant candy canes hanging from the evergreen trees. The top third of the trees were vacant, but no matter.

"Help me with this," she said. They carefully wrapped lights around each support post. The boys held the strands while Carli went up and down the step stool. With one connection needed to plug the extension cord in, it was show time.

"Are you ready?" she asked. "Ta-da!"

It was beautiful. Wide smiles covered all their faces as they moved out into the yard to admire their work. She thumbed Lank's name again but still no answer. She clicked off, pocketed the phone, and then it buzzed. That must be Lank.

"We are trying to locate Lank Torres."

"This is his wife. Can I help you?"

"Mrs. Torres, this is the kennel, and we are housing a dog for Kelly Reynolds. We've had a power outage and cannot keep their dog. We'll need someone to come get him."

Good grief. Where was Lank?

"We are on our way. Can you give me that address?" She clicked END and then texted Lank asking him to call her ASAP. "Let's go, guys. We have to pick up your dog."

As she turned to go back inside to find her car keys, she heard a thud and a scream followed by Zane tearing around from the side of the house, tears streaking his face.

"My brother is hurt!"

Chapter Fifteen

Carli

Carli followed her nephew Zane around to the side of the house where Junior cradled his left arm, a candy cane beside him. The ladder had toppled to the ground and lay on one side on the brown grass. From the angle of his wrist, it looked broken. Carli pushed down the wave of nausea that made her stomach lurch, and focused on what she needed to do to help Junior. She had always heard to use a rolled-up magazine to support broken limbs.

"Stay there. Don't move." She ran back inside, grabbed a magazine and a dish towel. Carefully placing his arm in the magazine for stability, she tied the dish towel around his neck and helped him up. It was broken. No doubt about it.

She called Lola. "I think Junior broke his arm. Can you go to the ER with us? Do you know where Lank is?"

Barely clicking to end the call, Lola barreled out of the cookhouse with a purse in one hand and the other arm in her coat sleeve. She was at Junior's side in a minute.

Carli turned to comfort Zane who had frozen in place, tears streaming down his cheeks and sobs wracking his slight frame. "Is my brother going to die?" he whimpered.

"No, sweetie. He's not going to die, but we have to take him to the emergency room right now."

They piled into Carli's pickup truck, Lola's calm voice providing directions. A good thing since she couldn't for the life of her remember where the closest hospital might be. By now she could hear sniveling from the backseat, coming from the one who shouldn't be crying.

"Zane, calm down," Lola said. "We're almost to the hospital. He's going to be all right."

Carli took the turn into the hospital a bit too fast, which caused Junior to moan. Her heart dropped to her knees, and she felt tears prick the back of her eyes, but she didn't slow down. Pulling under the emergency portico, Lola jumped out first before the wheels had come to a complete stop, jerked open Junior's door, and helped him walk through the sliding doors.

Zane opened his door. "Hang on just a minute," Carli said. "I need to move in case an ambulance comes in."

She parked and they went inside, leaving a message for Lank as they walked.

They couldn't find Junior and Lola in the waiting area which was good. Maybe they had already taken him back to an exam room. Carli took a deep breath and tried Lank's number again. Still no answer. Aggravation made her belly ache.

"Ma'am, are you with the young boy? You can come with me. They're waiting on x-rays."

A nurse greeted her with a friendly smile. Carli clenched Zane's hand and they followed the nurse through more double sliding glass doors into a room with curtained cubicles.

"Number three." She pointed.

Junior looked so small sitting on the ER bed, his face pale and his arm still propped by the magazine. Lola sat in the chair next to the bed.

"How are you doing?" Carli asked. "Are you in much pain?"

An orderly appeared with a wheelchair, and they helped Junior out of bed and then wrapped a blanket around his legs.

"We'll be back in a jiff," the orderly said.

Junior turned sad, pleading eyes to Carli but kept a brave face as he was wheeled away. Making an effort to keep her face calm, she gave him a reassuring smile. "You'll do fine. It'll be okay."

But on the inside, her heart was in her throat, and she could not get that image of a twisted wrist out of her head.

"I guess I should try to call his mother. What time is it in England?" Carli tapped her phone to find a universal clock. "And I still can't get a hold of Lank."

Silence fell on the room as they waited to hear about results of the x-ray. Zane climbed into Carli's lap. She wrapped an arm tightly around him, her heart warmed. He was one upset little boy and obviously worried about his big brother.

Carli's phone beeped and she tugged it out of her pocket. Finally, Lank must be in range where her messages all came through.

"I'm looking for Lank Torres."

"This is his wife. Can I help you?"

"Mrs. Torres. We've been trying to reach him all day. This is the kennel, and we have Kelly Reynold's dog. Someone else may have tried calling you. A water main has flooded, and we cannot take care of the animals. We need you to come get him right away."

Carli's mind went blank. "Get the dog? Are you sure you have the right number? Wait, someone did call earlier. I'm sorry. We're dealing with a hospital emergency." She held the phone, then asked the little one, "Zane, do you have a dog?"

"Yes, Brute. His name is really Tiny Brute, but we call him Brute."

Back into the phone, she said to the kennel person, "If you can text an address to this number, I'll be there as soon as I can."

Where in the world was Lank?

Chapter Sixteen

Mandy

The morning flew by and, despite her exhaustion, Mandy completed all of Calvin's requests and then some. She even helped the cook put away groceries in the small café that served their customers on sale days. Calvin had talked about opening up the dining room for other days, but he wasn't willing to hire help which meant Mandy would be the one filling in if the fry cook got swamped. No, thank you. She had enough jobs on her plate. And the worry of how she would deal with a little one *and* keep her job engulfed her body in tides of weariness and despair. She forced herself to push those thoughts from her mind.

Her grandmother always told her to pray without ceasing and to pray about all things, but she was past the point of God helping her. She had made so many bad decisions of late. Now she had to cowgirl up and face the consequences.

There had been some good news that surfaced in her world recently. Calvin announced that the sale barn would be closing for the holidays through the first of the year. That meant she would have the baby in a few weeks and wouldn't have to come back to work until January. The bad news was that some of that time would be without pay, and she didn't know if he would let her stay at the sale barn. There was no way she could afford an apartment right now.

"Calvin. I'm headed out."

"Where? It's not quitting time."

"Remember, I have a doctor's appointment this afternoon. I can't miss it. You said I could have the afternoon off, and I've done all the work you needed."

"Whatever," he waved an arm over his head, the scowl on his face remained, but he didn't say anything further.

She loved her job at the sale barn, and for the most part Calvin was an okay boss, but he had become so dependent on her. It was because she knew the business inside and out. Not just for the fact that she was good with numbers, but she could handle the fussy cowboys too. She spoke their language and they always came to her to settle their disputes. She used to go to Calvin with their complaints and issues, but he just made things worse. Now she made the decisions and Calvin was happy because he didn't have to deal with it.

That all changed when she had had an affair with the new auctioneer. Her coworkers lost respect for her. She could tell they looked at her differently. It would take several more years before she earned it back, but she was determined to make this sale barn one of the most successful in the Texas Panhandle. The local farmers and ranchers knew her and believed she would always treat them right. They trusted this operation which was why they kept bringing their livestock back time and time again.

In the ladies' room she changed her shirt and brushed the dust off her pants. Leaning over, she ran her fingers through the mess that grew on the top of her head and called it good. She had used the last of the hairspray two weeks ago. A dusting of face powder helped to even out her blotchy complexion, and a swipe of pink lip gloss did wonders.

Pregnancy had really changed her body. No one ever tells you that. In the beginning, her face had glowed, but now her skin was pale and dark circles glared at her from under each eye. Concealer didn't help. She had tried.

Grabbing her purse and waving at Candace in the office, Mandy walked outside to a glorious afternoon. The air nipped her nose and made her fingers tingle. Her heart felt light at the idea of seeing her son again on the exam screen and hearing his heartbeat on the monitor. There was nothing like that sound in the world.

The door of her faded blue car squeaked as she opened it and rummaged through the pile of junk in the backseat. Where was that nicer coat? It wouldn't cover her belly, but it didn't smell of cow manure and dust. Slipping the coat on, she squeezed in behind the steering wheel and pulled the door shut with a clunk. She turned the key. Nothing. Pursing her lips, she turned it over again. Nothing. "No. Juanita, don't do this to me."

Yes, she was one of those crazy girls who named her car. Juanita fit perfectly. There had been a reason she and her friends had come up with the name, probably based on a silly joke or adventure, but that seemed eons ago. She wished she could remember.

Placing her hands on the steering wheel, she thought about options. All the cowboys had already gone home for the day, and her boss Calvin did not need to know what a pathetic state of affairs her life was in right now. It was enough that she had to sleep in the storeroom. She did not want him to take her to the gynecologist too. That would make things really weird.

Lank's face suddenly flashed in her mind. Without hesitation, that was all she needed to punch his number in. She still recalled it, and hopefully he hadn't blocked her. But no, he wouldn't do a thing like that. He wasn't that type of guy.

"Hey." His voice deep and confident. At one time the sound had made her heart flutter, but not anymore.

"Lank?"

There was hesitation with his return answer and then a hint of confusion. "Yes?"

"I am sorry to bother you. This is Mandy. My car will not start, and I really need help."

"What's wrong with it?"

"I have no idea. It won't even turn over."

"Sounds like a battery. Are you at the sale barn?"

"Yes. I know it's a bit of a drive for you, but there is really no one else I can call. I have a doctor's appointment I cannot miss. I hope I didn't catch you at a bad time."

"Actually, I'm headed into Dixon for a tractor part. I'll just pass through town and head up your way. Be there in a few."

"Lank. This really means a lot to me."

"No problem."

She glanced at her watch to calculate the time. She could just make her appointment if they hurried. While she waited, she went back inside to use the restroom again. Slipping in the side door so that Calvin couldn't see her from his office, she calmed herself and tried to clean up a bit more. Checked her makeup again and wiped the dust from her boots with a wet paper towel. By the time she made it back to her car, Lank was pulling into the parking lot.

She waved and he waved back, pulling to a stop next to her car; he rolled down his window.

"Want me to take a look under the hood?"

"Is it okay if we leave? I really can't miss this appointment, and we're running a little late."

"Sure. Hop in." His smile was warm and genuine. Her heart warmed at his kindness.

"Where to?" he asked.

"It's just one town over. Dr. Hendricks in Pampa."

"How are you feeling?"

"Big as a whale, but I'm anxious to meet the little guy. How is married life treating you?"

"It's good."

"Where did you go on your honeymoon?"

"We didn't. We got hitched and went right back to work. Carli is intense and a workaholic like me. She'd rather be lunging a horse than sitting on a beach somewhere." He chuckled.

"I'm really glad you found someone, Lank. I wish you all the best."

"Thanks, Mandy. I wish the same for you, and you'll find him one day. When you least expect it. I wasn't looking for Carli and then there she was."

"I'm happy with my little man here."

"What's his name?"

"I have a few ideas, but I want to see him first and then I'll know for sure."

Lank cleared his throat. "I guess Jeff is out of the picture?"

Hearing his name sent a sharp sting to her heart, and she stifled the surprise that Lank knew. Then again, typical with a small town. With her naivete, she thought she and Jeff had been keeping things on the down low. But, of course, everybody probably knew about her situation, and everybody had also known about his wife and kids. Everybody except her.

"I never told him. He took the job in Oklahoma and took his wife and kids instead of me. End of story."

Lank didn't respond. Just listened.

"It sounds so stupid now," she said. "But I never knew he had a family. They lived in Amarillo, and he drove back and forth to the sale barn."

"I admire you for raising this baby on your own."

"Yeah, well, all men are lying pigs except this one." She touched her stomach. "This boy is going to grow up to having manners and be good and kind. Just like my dad."

"Your dad was a good man. I really liked him."

"He always liked you too. In fact, he liked all my friends from school."

"Saddest day ever when he passed. I still remember the funeral. Have you talked to your mom, lately?"

"Not since that blow up at the football game. In front of the whole town. I'm not even sure what I did. I know I was a little wild. She had to save face with her friends, and I got tossed out."

"I don't remember it going down like that," said Lank. "Your mom is a patient and understanding lady. I always liked her too."

"Mothers and daughters. Water under the bridge. You can turn in right there and park in the lot behind this building." Mandy pointed the way, thankful to be done with the walk back through memory lane. She wasn't fixating on the past anymore. She was only looking towards the future.

"Is it okay if I drop you off? Thought I might check the parts store here and see if they have what I need for the tractor while you're in the doctor's. I'll be waiting for you when you get done."

Mandy put a smile on her face. "Sure. Thanks, Lank."

Inside, her heart fell. She was going to ask him to go in with her. For nine months she'd been going to the doctor, watching the waiting room fill with couples who shared their love and joy. It would have been fun to show Lank the monitor and introduce him to her son.

Maybe this was a joy meant for just her, and no one else. That was okay. She could handle it.

Chapter Seventeen

Carli

Carli stood in her nephew's hospital room, staring at her phone. Her mind numb, she had to find Lank. He needed to be here with Junior, or he should be dealing with his sister's dog.

Panic and guilt washed over her. How would she ever explain to her sister-in-law about the broken bone? It was her fault. And Lank should be here. Her insides trembled but she couldn't tell if it was from worry that something might have happened to him or from anger.

"Lank is still not answering. I guess Buck is with him." Carli glanced up at Lola while she clicked on Lank's name one more time.

"No. Buck took Fancy to the vet," Lola said. "She was colicky all through the night and Buck tried everything. He's worried about her."

"He can't come get you then. I have to pick up the dog, but I hate to leave you and Junior here by yourselves."

"Don't worry," Lola said. "We'll be here another two hours or more by the time they read the x-rays and set the arm. I'm praying he doesn't need surgery."

Carli's insides cringed. She hadn't thought of that.

"There might be a snag with the paperwork," said Lola. "I can't sign everything, but if you can find Lank in the meantime, he'll have to drop by here."

"If you don't mind my abandoning you, I'll go get the dog and take him back to the ranch, then hurry back here to pick up you and Junior."

"We'll be fine. After they set his arm, I bet they'll let us watch television for a bit until you get here. I'll stay with him." Lola was always so reassuring.

Carli had to deal with this so she might as well get started. She leaned down and gave Lola a hug. "Thanks. I owe you one."

"No problem. Glad I can help."

"Let's go, Zane, you're coming with me." As he sprawled on the bed, she motioned towards the door.

"I want to stay here and watch TV, too."

"I know you're worried about your brother, but I need your help with the dog. What if I bring the wrong one home? What if he refuses to come with me?"

He looked longingly at the television for another minute and then glanced at Carli with worry in his eyes. With a heavy sigh, he swung his legs over the side of the bed and stood.

"We'll be back as soon as we can."

"You're walking too fast," Zane complained.

Carli felt like she should find the x-ray department and at least let Junior know they were leaving. She read the signs to find the way.

Her phone buzzed. "This is the kennel. You must come get this dog. We are sorry for the inconvenience, but we just can't keep him."

"I understand. I'm on my way." *Was that like the third time they called? These people are persistent.* She shook her head.

With that she turned down the next hall that pointed to the nearest exit. "Now what is your dog's name again?"

"Tiny Brute, but we call him Brute. Can I have a burger?"

Carli glanced at her cell phone. Good grief, it was after lunch. Frustrated, she punched Lank's name again leaving a detailed message about the morning's events. With Zane buckled in, she checked texts for the kennel address which they had not sent, so she called them back and then punched the address into her phone's map app. It was on the far side of Amarillo, of course. She hated to drive off and leave Lola without a vehicle, but there was no other option. And once again her emotions were a jumble in her belly. She didn't know if Lank was hurt or if she'd have to hurt him when she saw him next.

She spied the drive-in at the same time Zane did. "There! I want a large," he shouted with excitement.

"Okay, a large what?"

"May I take your order?" came out of the speaker.

"One moment, please. Zane, what do you want? A cheeseburger?"

"No."

"That's what you said. Chicken strips? Corn dog?"

"I want a suicide."

"One large suicide slush. Anything else?" the voice box asked.

"No. Wait. What's a suicide?"

"A suicide, ma'am, includes every slush flavor."

"No. Pick one flavor and make it a small. What

do you want to eat?" Carli's patience was wearing thin. Her phone buzzed and she recognized the kennel number again, but no Lank. *That has to be a mistake. Those people cannot be calling me again.*

"Hurry and decide, Zane. There are cars behind us."

Silence.

"I need a kid's meal with a cheeseburger, fries." She ordered a chicken strip wrap as well.

"I want a suicide," the little voice from the back came.

Carli gave in, just because the look on his face was so pitiful and his morning had been just as rough as hers. "And one suicide slush, small. That's all."

After their food was paid for, she pulled off the street into the next business's parking lot and climbed out to unpack the food. Zane's car seat had a cup holder. How convenient.

"Here drink this and don't spill it, okay?"

Zane took a long draw from the straw and squinted his face.

"It's good," he said.

Carli laughed.

"We didn't get ice cream!" Zane announced just before he stuffed his face with a huge bite of burger.

"I didn't know we were supposed to get ice cream. That will have to wait for another day."

The thought suddenly occurred to her that wherever Lank might be, Colton might be there too. So, she punched Colton's number before pulling into traffic. His phone rang ten times, but no answer. It was obvious his message box had never been set up. Typical. No surprise.

They followed the loop around the north side of

the city and took an exit off into a neighborhood with rolling, manicured lawns surrounding impressive homes. The road wound around and past several properties until she came to a sign at the end of the blacktop—KENNEL.

"This must be the place." She pulled to a stop in front of a red barn. "Go with me, Zane. Your dog may not come to me."

They went through a door marked OFFICE.

"Are you here for Tiny?" a frazzled young woman asked as she pushed her hair behind one ear. "Finally! I'm sorry to have called so many times. It's just that we're having a crisis."

Before Carli could answer, the lady spun on her heel and disappeared behind a door. Carli heard clanging and a shout and then the door opened to the rush of the most beautiful tri-colored dog she had ever seen, dragging the woman behind him. He skidded to a stop when he spotted them.

"Brute," said Zane. "Come here, boy."

The dog looked at him and then back at the handler.

"This is Tiny Brute?" asked Carli.

"He's a Bernese Mountain Dog," the vet assistant explained. "From the Swiss Alps. They love cold weather. Tell Kelly we're sorry but we had a main water line that busted, and we have no way to water these animals. Sorry for the inconvenience. I tried Kelly's number several times."

"She is actually in Europe. I'm Carli, her sister-in-law. Will he get in my car?" she asked, nodding to Brute who, it appeared by his stiffness and stare, hadn't quite decided to trust her yet.

"Oh, sure. It takes a while for them to warm up

to you. They only bond with one person."

"He's my dad's dog," Zane said.

"Thanks." The woman handed the leash to Carli. "Y'all have a nice day. I have to get back to our plumbing issue." With that she disappeared again behind the door, leaving Carli and Zane to handle the dog.

"Zane, you open the car door and call him. Can you do that for me?" Carli held out her hand for Brute to sniff, which he did. At least he didn't take off her fingers. But he refused to follow. She tried to drag him and was glad he wore a harness so that she wouldn't choke him by the neck. Holding the door open, she said, "Call him, Zane."

"Here, boy. Come on, Brute," shouted Zane.

"Let's go, boy," Carli tried.

In the next instant, thank God, Brute made up his own mind and it was all Carli could do to hang on. With one graceful leap he was in the car. Carli picked up Zane and had him buckled in before the dog could change his mind. Carli walked around the car and jumped into the driver's seat. She worried that the dog might rush the door when it opened, and she'd have no way to stop him.

Sitting on the backseat next to Zane, the dog gave her a curious look, as though he were saying, "Who are you and where are we going?"

"I guess we could put him in the barn?"

"He sleeps in Mom and Dad's room. He's not an outdoor dog." Zane reached out a tentative hand to give Brute a pat on his back.

"Oh great," Carli said as she drove a tad over the speed limit through the neighborhood to get back to the interstate. Where could she put Brute?

Lank sure had a lot of explaining to do.

Chapter Eighteen

Carli

Tiny Brute seemed content watching the world pass by out the side window as Carli sped towards ranch headquarters. He was content until he wasn't, so indicated by a leap from the backseat into the front passenger seat.

"Whoa!" she said. "Okay then."

"That's where Daddy lets him ride," noted Zane.

"It would have helped to have known that before now," said Carli. Brute took up the entire seat and his head reached the top of the cab.

She was never so glad to see the Wild Cow Ranch headquarters in her life. She buzzed down the hill and came to a stop in front of her house and started to open her door. But before she could shout "No," Brute had bumped her leg aside and sailed out the driver's door and taken off for the corral. About that time, her ranch foreman parked his truck and livestock trailer next to the barn. Carli took off running after the dog.

"Buck!" Carli saw him shutting a gate at the corral. "I left Lola and Junior at the hospital. Do you have any idea where Lank is?"

"Whoa now. What's all the fuss about?"

"Did you happen to see the dog that just went by?"

"I thought it was one of those little brown bears from New Mexico." He laughed.

"Nope. That's Kelly and Matt's dog, and he's staying here too. Junior fell off the ladder and broke his arm, so I need to go back to the hospital and pick him up. Lola's with him."

"All right. You go to the hospital, and I'll take Zane here with me to round up that critter. Where's he staying?"

"I guess with us. He's an indoor dog." Carli shot a glance at Zane.

Buck raised an eyebrow with a perplexed look on his face but didn't say anything else.

"Zane, help Buck find Brute. I'll be back soon."

With that she hurried back across the compound, jumped into her truck, and sped back up the hill towards town. What a day. Whatever had her husband occupied for an entire day was going to take some explaining.

Pulling into the hospital Carli went through the sliding doors and past the empty front desk. Someone, a volunteer probably, had cranked up the popcorn machine. The smell reminded her of the downtown movie theatre in Atlanta. She should drag Lank to the movies sometime. And then she remembered the burger she and Zane had eaten while Lola and Junior were still here. They must be starving by now.

She hurried to the emergency room they had been in and pushed back the curtain, but it was empty. The bed linens all tight and clean, ready for the next patient. There was no one at the nurses' station either. Following the signs she wondered about the cafeteria, and there they were.

Junior's arm was in a sling with a brand-new cast. Lola watched him eat ice cream while she sipped a cup of coffee.

"There you guys are. Junior, are you okay?"

Junior shrugged his shoulders and kept eating, although his eyes did light up for a minute when he saw her.

"Did you get the dog?" asked Lola.

"Yes. The dog has been delivered and Buck and Zane are running after him as we speak." Carli laughed, because she really felt like crying but that wouldn't solve anything.

"What's next? Are they releasing him to go home?" She wanted to get this day back under control.

"Yes, but they need some signatures. Wonder if his mom can be reached by phone in Europe?" Lola asked. "They just need her permission."

"What about his grandmother? I completely forgot about her. Maybe Kelly gave her mother authority to sign for the boys. Junior, do you know where your grandma is?"

"I dunno. Maybe on a cruise. She likes those. I can't remember," he answered between bites.

"I'll go to the office and see what I can do."

While Carli walked back down the hall, she punched Lank's number again. His voice surprised her. "Lank! Where are you?"

"Busy. I'll tell you later. Looks like you've called me more than once today." A tinge of annoyance in his voice.

"Yes, I have," she answered and didn't hide the annoyance in her reply. "Your nephew broke his arm. The dog ran away. We need your signature on the paperwork. I'm at the hospital. How soon can you be here?"

"Okay, okay. Take a breath. I'm on my way."

She stood under the portico of the emergency entrance, pacing back and forth not realizing how tense she felt until she saw the sight of Lank's truck. Relief washed over her like a waterfall. Where had he been all day? She half-ran out to the parking lot to confront him as he opened the pickup truck door.

"We have to go to the business office. Have you heard from your sister? Do you know if she can get a phone call?"

"Easy with the questions. Take a breath." He put his hands on her shoulders. "Yes, I can fill out the paperwork for my nephews. She gave me a power of attorney just in case they needed medical treatment." He rummaged through his glove box. "How did he break his arm? Which nephew?"

"Junior was helping me with decorations. He fell off the ladder." Carli couldn't even begin to explain how horrible she felt, and that it was all her fault for not watching him closer. How would they ever tell Kelly? Should they wait until she gets home, or would she want to know now? Since it was Lank's family, Lank could be the bearer of bad news, Carli decided.

They walked back inside and Lank had the paperwork completed to everyone's satisfaction. Within another half hour, they were walking to the parking lot.

"I want to ride with Uncle Lank," said Junior.

They climbed back into their vehicles, and as they drove away, Carli realized she never found out where Lank had been. She forgot to ask, and he didn't offer the information. She turned and looked at Lola.

"Wonder where Lank was all day?" she murmured.

"He didn't tell me," said Lola. "Buck may have given him a job to do."

Lola didn't seem to be as curious or as concerned as Carli was. They rode in silence back to Wild Cow Ranch headquarters. By the look on Lola's face, Carli could tell she was exhausted.

"Thanks, Lola. I couldn't have made it through this day without you," Carli said.

"I'm thinking it might take all four of us to keep up with these boys over the next couple of weeks."

"I'm afraid that you might be right," said Carli.

Lank's truck was already parked in front of their house. Carli dropped Lola off at her back door, and then drove around to park in her own driveway. She hurried inside to confront Lank, but then realized any discussion they had would have an audience.

Junior was resting on the couch, watching television, Zane was sitting on the floor, balancing a bowl of ice cream in his lap, and Brute filled the easy chair with his front paws resting on the ottoman.

"Why is it so cold in here?" Carli asked, as she hung her purse on the back of a dining room chair.

"Brute has to have it cool. If he gets too hot, he gets sick," Junior answered. "Trust me. You don't want him to throw up."

"Can he go outside?"

"No. He likes to stay with us," Zane said.

Carli wandered back to their bedroom to find Lank putting on fuzzy slippers. She plopped on the bed beside him.

"So. Tell me about your day," she said, making an effort to tap down any angry words.

"I had to help a friend."

"Who?"

He hesitated for much longer than she thought necessary, which only made her more suspicious. "Mandy."

Carli's fury burned to the surface, and underneath that was a memory of a past boyfriend kissing her rival. That guy and Lank were completely different, but she couldn't help the past hurt and utter rejection that flooded her brain. Rather than say something she'd regret, she remained silent.

"I can tell by the look on your face that you're very angry," Lank said. "She called and her car wouldn't start. I went to the sale barn to help, but she had a doctor's appointment that she couldn't be late for. So, I took her to Pampa."

"You never once answered my texts or calls? Why?" It was all that she could do not to raise her voice, but she kept it low because the boys were just down the hall in the living room.

"I swear that I didn't get your messages. While she was at the doc's, I went to the parts store. I called you as soon as all those texts blew up my phone."

"Are you seeing her again?"

"No. Well, maybe. I couldn't figure out what's wrong with her car. Colton is going to help me tomorrow."

Carli folded her arms across her chest and sat there, tears brimming to the surface clogging her throat with emotion. Lank kneeled on the floor in front of her.

"I'm sorry. I know you had your hands full today. Thanks for handling everything. Mandy needs a friend right now, but that's it. There's nothing more between us. I love you. I married you."

She believed him, but there was still a niggling of doubt in her mind. It wasn't Lank that she didn't trust.

Chapter Nineteen

Carli

Newspapers spread across the dining room table, and green garland needles and sprigs fluttered all over the floor. Lily Jane picked up one branch in her mouth and ran around shaking it.

"Put it down, now!" Carli shouted. "Bad dog!"

Lank came into the room where Carli was attempting to assemble a Christmas wreath.

"Whoa, what's goin' on, babe? Why so mean to L.J.?"

"Her name is Lily Jane." Carli's face was red.

The medium-sized Border Collie tucked her tail, dropped the greenery from her mouth, and cowered near a chair.

"I've never seen you be so harsh with her. What's really goin' on?" He stood over her and laid a hand on her shoulder, then took a seat.

"We've been invited to dinner. Tonight. At Taylor Miller's." Her eyes filled with tears, but her mouth pursed with determination not to lose it at this moment.

"Well, that's great, babe. Isn't it? And why do you

say his whole name? He's your birth father."

"I don't know. I'm not going to call him Dad."

"Maybe one day you will. Anyway, why are you upset with Lily Jane, and what's the problem with going to dinner?"

She sighed and tried to release all the negative thoughts from her mind. "There's just so much to do. The Christmas decorations. Soon, baking cookies. Who knows? I might burn them." She grabbed a piece of garland and smashed it on the table. "And this stupid wreath. I don't know what I'm doing. I have no idea how to make one. Lily Jane is going crazy and thinks everything is a game. And now I'm supposed to smile and make nice-nice at dinner with Taylor Miller and his family? Sorry. I'm whining."

"Oh, Carli. Babe. You take on too much and you're too hard on yourself. Listen. L.J. is still a young pup so you gotta forgive her games. That's number one. Look at her. She's afraid. So, you'll have to make up with her. Two, so what if you don't know how to do everything? You ask for help. As far as baking cookies, make it fun with the other ladies. Lola, Belinda, Angie. They won't let you burn anything. Same with the wreath making. Get help. And as for dinner, let's just be open. Let's go. They're nice people. He's reaching out to you. We can do this together."

She looked at her husband. Married not quite a month.

"How did you get to be so wise?" she asked him.

"I dunno. Born this way? You forgot about handsome." He let out a laugh.

"I love you, Lank. Sorry. I am in such a funk."

"Now apologize to L.J."

"Please. Call her Lily Jane." She held out her hand to the dog who sniffed her fingers. Then Carli scooped her up and cuddled her in her lap although the dog was getting pretty big now. "I'm sorry, girl. Mommy was a tyrant. But you still can't eat the garland."

"That's right. We don't want any green poop."

"Lank!" She stretched out his name when she scolded him. But then they both joined in a hearty laugh.

During their entire conversation, Tiny Brute watched from the easy chair. Make that *his* easy chair, with giant paws and head almost covering the entire ottoman.

Carli took a deep breath and tackled the wreath again. She tried several different arrangements, encircling the woven grapevine with different combinations of sprigs and greenery. Taking apart several of her grandmother's old, dusty wreaths had resulted in a good pile of material. With the dust washed off, it could look new, and she wanted something cheery for the front door. In frustration, she dumped everything off the wreath for a third time. Less is more, she decided.

Taking an oversized candy cane, she wired that to one side. She tied a bow and glued a black and white gingham ribbon to the center of the cane. Added two sprigs of greenery and was done. It looked okay for an amateur. After hanging it on the front door, she stepped back to admire her work. Candy canes were her favorite.

Two sleepy heads appeared in the entry hall.

"Did our mom email last night?"

"Let's look. We read before that they made it," said Carli. "Come on."

Both boys and both dogs padded behind her. She opened her computer and sure enough, there was an email from Kelly in her In-box. Zane climbed into her lap. She read it out loud to the boys.

Hi Everyone!

Just a quick email for now.

The airline lost our luggage. Or misplaced it for a while. The first night we didn't have our pajamas! What do you think of that, boys? LOL.

Luckily, the next morning the hotel people knocked on our door and delivered our suitcases. Yay! Now we have clean clothes and our own toothbrushes.

Boys, are you brushing your teeth for Aunt Carli? I sure hope so. We don't want to come home to smelly breath and dirty teeth. LOL.

Signing off for now . . .

LOVE YOU WITH ALL OUR HEARTS!

Mom

"Of all the things she could tell us about Europe, she tells us to brush our teeth?" Junior folded his arms across his chest and stared at the screen with a frown.

Carli had to laugh. "She must miss you guys."

Lank appeared at her back and leaned over to read the email. "Is that from my sister?"

"Maybe you should answer her and tell her you need to talk to her on the phone." Carli turned to glare at him.

"Naw. It's probably nighttime there," he said.

"You have no idea what time it is in Europe," Carli said. "Lank Torres. You get back here."

"Buck and I are going to get started on lights today," he called out from the kitchen. "Just like you want."

That boy did not take instruction very well, probably because she kept nagging at him, but she was not going to talk to his sister. He should be the one to do that.

"I wish Mom would come back. Dad too." Zane turned big, sad eyes to Carli. He must be very homesick. She clicked off the computer. Time for a little distraction. "What does your dog eat? Is he house trained? I just have so many questions. I'm not sure how to take care of him so I need you guys to help me. Can you do that?"

They both nodded their heads.

"Good. Get dressed, I'll fix you a quick breakfast and then we'll take the dogs outside for some fresh air. Lank and I have a dinner tonight to go to, so I need to see if Lola can watch you guys for a while."

With everybody back in motion and occupied, Carli took a deep breath. They had to get word to Kelly about Junior in some way. But she had no idea what the best way would be without coming completely unglued over the situation.

With coats and hats on, everybody spilled out into the front yard. The very first thing Tiny Brute did was take off towards the creek with Lily Jane in hot pursuit. Maybe they could keep each other out of trouble. The boys wandered out to the road to watch Buck and Lank string lights. Before Carli made it across the compound, both boys had a job holding the strands to keep the tangles out.

"Lola! Are you here?" Carli called out as she walked into the two-story cookhouse. The bottom floor was a dining hall, oversized kitchen, and pool table room. The second floor had several spare bedrooms for cowboys when they worked at branding, plus a foreman's apartment where Buck and Lola lived. They had a tiny space, with a small kitchen, master bedroom and bath, and a small living room. Lola had decorated it based on her Mexican heritage, with brightly colored walls, terra cotta, heavy wooden furniture, and leafy plants.

"In here," Lola answered.

On the granite island, Lola had spread out parchment paper. About half of the area was covered in cookies.

"Those look delicious," Carli said.

"Thought I'd get a start on the cookies for the Open House. These are simple sand dollars, is what we call them. Help yourself."

Carli couldn't resist. The soft, buttery cookie melted in her mouth.

"That hasn't been rolled in powdered sugar yet. Try one of those, and then wash your hands and roll up your sleeves. You can help."

"I'd love to help." Eager to learn everything Lola could teach her, Carli hurried back from the sink, drying her hands just as Lola pulled a batch from the oven.

"Get those tongs and roll these in that bowl of powdered sugar." Lola showed her how with the first one and then Carli got to work.

"I have a huge favor." Carli glanced at Lola to judge her reaction. Lola didn't look up from the mixing bowl. "Lank and I have been invited to the Millers for dinner and I was wondering if you could watch the boys."

"Of course. Don't think another thing about it. They can even sleep over here, if that helps. Might distract them a bit. I'm sure they're missing their parents."

"I thought Zane was going to bust out crying a while ago. Poor kid."

Lola walked closer to Carli and put an arm around her shoulder. "I know this must be difficult, but I am so happy that Taylor has reached out to you. Give him a chance."

"You're the second person that's told me that," Carli said.

"Sometimes God speaks through others and guides you in new directions. All you have to do is follow the lead." Lola squeezed her waist.

Carli had dreamed about meeting her birth father her entire life, and now that she knew him, her heart thudded in her chest at the idea of going to his home. What do you talk about to a man whose blood flows in your veins, but who knows absolutely nothing about you?

"I don't even know what to say to him. I'm glad Lank is going too. Where do we even start, Lola?"

"You start with dinner."

Chapter Twenty

Taylor

At the Millers' house Karissa was setting the table and Taylor was dicing tomatoes and onions.

"I wish the kids could've stayed home tonight and joined us," he said.

"Maybe it's better this way. It'll give the four of us time to get to know one another better. We already have enough drama to deal with Shayla as it is."

"I guess you're right."

He was nervous. Not exactly sure why. Oh, right, getting together with a daughter he never knew he had. Twenty-eight years. Made him sad to think of Carli alone all those years. Of course, she had foster parents, but he had heard they weren't that involved. They were older and passed away. Pretty much raised herself. What would life have been like if he could've been her father? Well, they had now. What would they do with it? Could they have a friendship? A relationship? This was a first step. Dinner with Carli and her newlywed husband, Lank. Well, maybe her wedding and their dance at the reception was the first step. So, this was the second. One step at a time.

"Onions and tomatoes are diced, darlin'."

"Put the onions in a little bowl. Not everyone likes them in their salad. Thanks, sweetie."

Taylor heard a truck engine outside and looked to the window. He hurriedly washed his hands. "They're here."

Karissa came over and touched his arm. "Take a breath. Everything will be fine."

"I know." He inhaled deeply. "I just want her to feel comfortable."

"She will. Now go let them in."

Taylor went out the side door and through the garage.

"Hey! Welcome. Come in this way. No one uses the front door much." He was all grins.

Lank stepped up to shake his hand. "Thanks for having us, Taylor."

"Sure. Sure thing. Come on in." Not sure whether he should hug Carli, he put a hand on her shoulder for a few seconds. "Glad I cleaned the garage, so you don't have to dodge boxes. We took some supplies to a women's shelter the other day." He was rambling. *Why are you nervous? Don't be a jerk.*

They all got inside, and Karissa said, "Hey! C'mon in. So nice to have you both. Can I get you some sweet tea?"

"Thank you, ma'am, that'd be great," Lank said, all smiles.

"Now you can call me Karissa. Please have a seat. We have some veggies if you want to start with those. Here are some little plates."

Taylor said to Lank with a grin, "And if you don't

want celery and carrots, try the fried jalapeño poppers. Made 'em myself."

"Don't mind if I do, thanks."

"Now, Taylor, don't you lie," Karissa teased. "You got those at the store."

"Well, I put them in the oven, didn't I?"

Carli chuckled. "Sounds like you cook like I do."

"We've got something in common."

Taylor looked at Carli deeper than with just a little joke in his eyes.

"I'll put the steaks on the grill when we're ready. Now that's something I do know how to cook," he said.

Lank chuckled. "It's a guy thing."

"Now wait a minute," Carli interjected. "Don't go getting all sexist on us. Maybe it's something I could learn."

Taylor smiled. "And I would be honored to teach you."

"Fine." Lank smiled. "I'll just have me another one of these poppers. My compliments to the chef."

"Lank, you can help me if you want," Karissa said. "We can let those two handle the beef. If that's okay with you."

"Fine by me. Don't ever let it be said that I stood in the way of my wife and a slab of prime meat. Just don't let her burn mine!"

Taylor and Carli went outside carrying plates of four steaks that had been resting on the kitchen counter for about thirty minutes. Taylor said, "Don't take cold steaks from the fridge and put 'em right on the grill. You might end up with burned outside and raw inside."

After giving more tips, the grill was ready to

accept the meat.

"Now we gotta remember the orders we took. I think Lank likes his rare as though it was just on the hoof a few minutes ago." He grinned. "You and Karissa like yours a nice pink inside, medium rare. I like mine well done. I don't need to see blood on my plate."

"Ooh, yuck," she said.

"Four to five minutes to char. Then three to five minutes each side for medium rare. For Lank's we'll just wave the steak over the grill."

Deep laughs came out of both of them.

"Thanks for coming, Carli. It means a lot to me."

"Me too."

"Your wedding and reception were both very special. I told you there that I hope to make up for lost years. I really meant that. Is that okay with you?"

She looked at the ground and pushed the hair from her eyes. Then looked back at him. "Yes." But then added, "Is it okay with your kids?"

He flipped a steak over with tongs. "I guess it'll take time for all of us. I know it's a strange situation. But I think it'll be good for everyone. In the end. Do you want to give it a try?"

His face was warm from the grill. And so was his heart when she said, "Yes. I'd like to try."

Chapter Twenty-One

Carli

The four gathered around the Millers' long, mahogany dining room table. It was beautiful, all shiny from the varnish with a lighter colored wood ingrained. Taylor was at the head of the table nearest the kitchen. Karissa was at his left rather than all the way at the other end. Carli was at Taylor's right and Lank was next to her.

After they held hands and Taylor said the blessing, food was passed around. Steaks, salad, potatoes.

"Man, this is good." Lank was nearly immersed in his steak, gliding the fork through the juice and catching a piece of potato which was slathered with butter and sour cream. If he made any smacking sounds Carli was ready to kick him under the table. But she was glad he was enjoying it.

He looked at her and asked, "Did you grill mine?"

She winked at Taylor and said, "Yes, I did. All I had to do was wave it over the grill for a couple of seconds and it was done."

"That's funny, babe. But you know what? It's delicious so go ahead with your jokes."

Everyone laughed and Taylor said, "She's a good student."

At the end of the meal, Karissa asked, "Does anyone need anything else?"

"My goodness, not for me." Carli touched her stomach. "That was delicious."

"Glad you enjoyed it." Karissa smiled. "You and Taylor were the main chefs."

The men settled back in their chairs and pushed away from the table. Carli started to stand to help clear dishes when Karissa said, "No. Please sit. Relax. You're our guests. I'll just take some of the dishes away. Then we can have dessert."

Taylor asked, "Want me to start the coffee, darlin'?"

"I can get it, sweetie," she said.

Soon Karissa brought out a pan of Texas sheet cake. Lank's eyes doubled in size. "Wow, that looks so good! Maybe you could teach Carli how to make that."

Karissa smiled. "It's easy. Let me grab some ice cream. Vanilla okay with everyone?"

When they all started in on their desserts, Taylor took on a serious tone. "Carli, if you don't mind my asking, what was it like living with your foster parents? I've been curious."

"Sweetie," Karissa said, "she may not want to talk about them."

"It's okay. Really." Carli pushed her dessert plate away. "They were nice people. They provided for me. Allowed me to pursue my interest in horses by paying for riding lessons. I started horse showing."

Lank interjected, "But they dropped you off at the barn and you went with the other kids. I think you told me that the Fitzgeralds didn't even watch you in shows. Right?"

"Well, no, they didn't," she said. "They were older, and it was uncomfortable for them to sit in the bleachers all day. And they didn't like the concession food, hot dogs and stuff. They were on a special diet."

Lank mumbled, "Old people's diet."

"Don't be mean." Carli frowned at him.

"Sorry." Lank touched her hand.

Karissa asked, "How old were you when they died? That must've been hard."

"Eighteen," Carli said. "If I had been younger, I would have been placed with other foster parents. I had been working since I was about fifteen. Different jobs. Cleaning out stables. Babysitting. I always had a job. When the Fitzgeralds passed, they left me a little bit of money. I first got a tiny apartment, and later rented a little house with a barn. I lived there until I moved to Texas."

Taylor asked, "And you had a horse training business?"

Carli nodded. "Yes. I started a small one, then partnered with my trainer. He had always helped get me and my horse ready for shows. Eventually he and I trained other girls and their horses. We trailered them to shows. Our clients were mostly high school and college age. The business was actually pretty successful when a rival of mine decided to go after me and ruin everything."

Lank held her hand. "But look how it all turned out. You would've never met me if you had stayed in Georgia."

Carli smiled at him and squeezed his hand.

"True. Best decision I ever made was to move to Texas. I never imagined there might be a life for me somewhere else. And I believe God had a part in steering me in the right direction. And now I'm eating dinner with the man who gave me life." She looked at Taylor who was intently listening.

Lank nodded. "But it could've gone the other way. You might've taken one look at the Wild Cow and decided to sell, move back to Georgia, and not even give me a second look." He tilted his head playfully.

"Babe, I would always give you a second look." She smooched his lips.

"Ah, newlyweds." Karissa sighed. "I remember those days."

Taylor huffed a little in jest and grabbed his wife's hand. "What do you mean, darlin'? Aren't we still like newlyweds?"

"Hmmm . . . let's see." Karissa's eyes went heavenward as though she was counting. "It's been more than twenty years. But you're right, sweetie. We try to keep the spark alive."

Taylor gave her a kiss on the lips.

"Well, ain't we all a bunch of lovebirds?" Lank laughed as he took another big bite of the cake and ice cream.

Just then the side door from the garage opened and Shayla called out, "I'm home."

Taylor turned halfway in his chair and looked towards the kitchen. "In here, darlin'. We have guests."

Shayla's stilettos clicked on the kitchen floor as she came to the dining room and looked at the four faces—one in particular, Carli's. Shayla didn't smile. But Carli did.

"Come say hello, sweetie. You know Lank and

Carli." Taylor reached for his daughter's arm. Carli thought she saw some tension and hoped she wasn't the cause.

"Hello." Shayla's face was still unsmiling.

Karissa stood. "Hope you had a good day at work, sweetie. Why don't you join us for some cake?"

Shayla's shoulders sank. "Mom, you know I don't eat that stuff."

Taylor grinned but Carli thought he looked uncomfortable. "I don't get why women are always dieting," he said. "You're thin enough already, Shayla. You have nothing to worry about." He let out a little chuckle, but Karissa gave him a frown. Carli knew he was treading on thin ice mentioning diet or weight to a female.

"Dad, you have no clue. Women always have to watch their appearance." Shayla looked at Carli who had come to the dinner in jeans. Her good jeans, but jeans nevertheless.

"That's a really pretty dress." Carli wanted to try to become friends with the girl and hated the awkwardness in the room.

Shayla didn't answer and Carli's comment hung in the air.

Karissa was still standing and picked up some of the used dessert dishes to take to the kitchen. "Shayla, sit down. Please join us."

The girl looked at Carli and said, "I'm tired, Mom. I'm going to lie down. Plus, I've got to answer some emails."

"Do you feel all right?" her mother asked.

"I'm fine. Just tired." She turned to head upstairs as Carli said, "It was nice to see you, Shayla."

There was no answer. Maybe a mumble or grunt.

After his daughter was out of earshot, Taylor leaned in towards Lank and Carli and in a low voice said, "Sorry about that. Shayla's a little high maintenance."

His wife frowned and shushed him.

"What? What?" He held out his open palms. "Shayla would say the same thing about herself. We've all kidded about it. She doesn't like getting dirty." And then looking in Carli's direction with a smile, Taylor added, "Shayla's not a cowgirl."

Just then they heard an upstairs door shut a little too loudly.

"Great," Karissa said. "She probably heard you, Taylor."

Carli shifted in her seat and held Lank's hand tighter. "Gosh, I hope I'm not causing anyone discomfort. Maybe we should go."

"No, Carli. Please stay. It's just a strange situation and will take some time for everyone to get used to." Karissa's face seemed to hold so much compassion.

Another door sounded, this time the side kitchen door.

"I'm home!" Hud's voice bellowed.

Taylor smiled. "Okay. Let's see how it goes with our second child."

Chapter Twenty-Two

Carli

"C'mon in here, Hud. We've got company." The pride and love he had for his son were evident on Taylor's face, Carli thought.

"Pulling off my boots, Dad."

Karissa called to Hud as she made her way to the kitchen. "Out in the garage, right? Not on my floor."

"Yes, ma'am."

Carli noticed that everything in this household was said good naturedly. Except maybe for Shayla's hissy attitude, that is. But Carli didn't hold it against her. Just protecting her turf. Maybe Carli would have acted the same way if she had a normal family like this one. In her mind she put quotation marks around the word normal for she knew no family was normal. Whatever that really meant.

Hud entered the kitchen in his stocking feet, leaving his boots out in the garage. First thing he did was hug his mom, which Carli could see part of as she leaned forward in her chair. Then Karissa led him to the dining room. "You remember Lank and Carli," she said.

"Yeah, hey, how's it going?" The young man reached around Taylor's chair to grab hold of Lank's hand. He smiled at Carli and greeted her too. He was friendly. Was that it? Were guys and girls so different? It seemed to her that Shayla held more hurt feelings than Hud.

Taylor intercepted his son to give him a half hug. "Whew! Can't hug ya all the way, kiddo. You smell like a barn."

"Well, Dad, that's where I was all day. What do ya expect? I washed up some before I got home. Even changed my shirt. I'll shower after I eat."

They all shared a laugh, then Lank piped up. "How's it goin' at Cross Creek?"

"Good. I'm workin' with a young colt and he's really comin' along."

"Hud has always had a way with horses. He's his dad's son," Karissa said.

Taylor almost puffed up. "Started him at a young age. Probably two or three, he was on the back of a horse."

Carli took all of this in, imagining what their family had been like then—Taylor and Karissa, newly married, with a little boy they had adopted from a druggie mother that Taylor had previously married, and then a baby girl of their own, Shayla. All the birthday celebrations, school days, Halloween costumes, Christmases. One big, happy family. How did she fit into that storybook picture? Did she ever fit in? Anywhere?

She had to snap out of it. She had Lank now. He was her family.

Karissa smiled at Lank and Carli. "I'm sure the two of you will have your children on horses right away. Are you planning a big family?"

Carli almost spit the water she had just sipped, out of her mouth, then coughed. Lank gripped her hand. "Carli's not sure about having children. But we're talkin' about it." She could see the love in his eyes.

"Oh, I am so sorry." Karissa's face turned red. "How insensitive of me. It's really none of our business and I shouldn't have intruded like that."

Carli was a little surprised that she could muster up calmness and be transparent with these people. "It's okay. I just never thought of myself as mother material. It's not like I had a mother around in my life as a role model. Mrs. Fitzgerald didn't really count."

Taylor pursed his lips and looked down at the napkin on his lap for a second. "I'm sorry, Carli. Michelle messed up her own life. I wish she hadn't caused hurt in yours too."

Everyone was quiet for a few seconds, when Hud, who was rummaging in the kitchen, broke the silence. "I'm starving. Hey, Dad, I might flip a steak on the grill, okay?"

Taylor cleared his throat. "Uh, sure, Son. It'll heat up real quick. Need my help?"

"Naw, I got it."

Karissa went to the kitchen and pulled out some dishes and salad. "Want a potato, Hud? You could set it on the grill for a couple minutes to warm it up."

"Sure, Mom."

While mother and son were in the kitchen, Taylor looked at Carli and she timidly gazed into his eyes as he said, "Carli, I hope you can let go of the hurt Michelle caused. You're a brave, capable, young woman. And now you have Lank. I don't pray as much as my wife does but I pray you both will have much happiness in your new life together."

A tear formed in the corner of Carli's eye. "Thank you so much. That means a lot to me."

"Me too," Lank said. "Thanks."

Karissa returned and sat with them. "I wanted to ask about the little boys, your nephews. How's that going? Didn't you say their parents were in Europe?"

"Well, let's see . . . we've survived a broken arm, a giant slobbery dog has taken over our house, and some homesickness. I guess it's going pretty good." Carli smirked. "The only thing I can cook that they like is boxed mac and cheese. And we all agree on the hot chocolate at the B&R Beanery in Dixon. I think we went there twice in one day."

The four of them busted out laughing.

"What do they say about boys?" Karissa cleared the last few things off the table. "Boys will be boys and they're rowdy, that's for sure. And then they grow up and act the same, except they're in a man's body."

Carli couldn't stop her burst of laughter. "That's exactly how Lank is. One minute he's stern and tough with his nephews, and the next minute he's rolling around on the floor wrestling."

Hud joined them at the table with his plate of rare steak, potato, and salad. "What are ya sayin' about boys?"

"We're saying we love you rascals." Karissa stood over him and hugged his shoulders.

Carli watched Hud and saw the resemblance to his father. Tall and lean with kind eyes. She couldn't help but wonder if she had any of Taylor's traits, physical or otherwise.

Chapter Twenty-Three

Carli

As Karissa continued clearing the table, except for where Hud was eating his dinner, she touched Taylor's shoulder and said, "I'm going to run upstairs, see if Shayla's okay. Maybe I can coax her to come down."

"Okay, darlin'. Let me know if you need anything."

The four at the table continued talking while Hud chewed his steak. Lank asked if he liked his job at the Cross Creek Ranch.

"Real good. Great bunch. I'm learnin' a lot. 'Course I come home dead tired." Hud chuckled and kept at his plate.

"Oh, come on now," Lank teased. "You're younger than I am, and I work all day at the Wild Cow. Man up."

Hud smiled.

"That's why we have to feed him so much. Gotta keep fuel in that young body of his."

Carli saw Taylor's eyes light up. He was sure a proud papa.

It was at that moment that she heard something heavy drop upstairs and a high voice, but she couldn't make out what was said. Maybe just one word, "Mom." Uh oh. What was going on with Karissa and Shayla? *Hope it's not because of me.*

The men kept talking the next few minutes when Karissa and Shayla came down the stairs and into the kitchen. The two rooms opened to each other, and Karissa poked her head into the dining room. "Shayla and I are going to clean up. Carli, you want to come out here with us? I won't put you to work but you can sit at the counter and chat with us."

"Sure. You can also put me to work though." Carli liked this woman.

Karissa said, "Shayla, if you could load the dishwasher, that'd be a big help."

Shayla didn't smile or say a word. She placed dishes in the machine one after the other.

Carli heard a few sighs come out of the girl. *Oh boy, this isn't going to be easy.* But she had to try. "Shayla, that's a really nice boutique where you work."

"Yes, it's very upscale. Most of our clientele is quite wealthy. The clothes are very expensive." Shayla took a few breaths through her nose and let them out quick.

"When we were there, I saw so many beautiful dresses."

"But you just bought one dress at my store, didn't you? I remember y'all were calling our dresses 'rust' but the real name is much nicer—'paprika'. You ended up wearing that dress. Where did you buy the bridal dress?"

"Another day we went to Marilyn's Bridal Shop

in Dallas."

"You're kidding. I know that store. That's an old shop. I'm surprised the woman is still alive. My boss talks about that place all the time."

"Be kind, Shayla," Karissa reminded.

"What? What'd I say?" Shayla's face turned dark with a frown.

Carli was uncomfortable. "The woman and the shop are older, like you said, Shayla. But it was a quaint place, and she was so sweet."

Karissa continued putting a few things away. "Let's finish up, ladies. Then we can look at the Christmas decorations in the garage. I pulled some extras out to give you for your Open House."

"Thank you. But you don't have to give them to me," Carli said.

"It's fine. We've collected so many over the years and we don't even decorate that much anymore."

"Thanks. I appreciate it."

"I'd like to help decorate too, if you need it. Shayla, you could come too. It'll be fun."

"Mom, I might have to help get things ready at my work. I told you we're having our party the same day." Shayla half-rolled her eyes at Carli. And then she announced, "I'm going upstairs. I told you I was tired and had emails to check."

"All right, Shayla. I'll come up later before bed. I love you."

Carli said, "It was nice to see you, Shayla."

No answer. Maybe a mumble.

After Shayla was out of earshot, Karissa said, "I am sorry."

"No worries. It'll take time."

"I'll be praying."

"Me, too." Carli smiled.

The women went to the garage and Karissa pulled out some boxes marked "Carli". Somehow that warmed Carli's heart, to know that this woman had been thinking of her and wanted to help her. If only her own mother had been so caring.

"There are some light strands in here and Taylor checked them out, so we know they work. And red bows. Lots of stuff. Maybe you'll find something useful."

"This is great. Thanks so much." Carli touched the box.

"Mom!" from the kitchen. It was Hud. "Are the dishes in the dishwasher clean?"

Karissa sighed. "Boys. Excuse me for one second. He knows that I dislike yelling back and forth."

When Karissa left, Carli lifted the box of decorations designated for her and placed it closer to the garage opening. Lank could put it in their truck when they were ready to leave. She looked up at the shelves. It was all neatly organized. Probably Taylor's doing. Tools were evenly spaced on the pegboard hanging on the wall. Reins were looped on a hook. A basketball, bat, and glove rested in a netting. Maybe from days gone by or waiting for a pickup game with father and son.

An open box caught her attention. Photo albums. Not wanting to be a snoop but curiosity won out. Carli pulled one out and opened the white covered book. Baby pictures. Captions written with a gold pen—"Shayla", "Sweet girl". Turning more pages she saw a toddler, then a little girl on a bicycle with Taylor hovering over her.

"That boy." Karissa came back in and stood

behind her. "I put a magnet on the front that says clean or dirty."

The album was abruptly shut. "Oh, sorry. The box was open." Carli's eyes blinked hard.

"It's okay, Carli. I'm sorry. It must be very hard for you."

"I've gotten used to it over the years." There was that "tough soldier" façade. She was a little sick of it. Could she let this woman in? Or keep her at arm's length?

Karissa came closer. "I've learned through church and Bible studies about the love of God. Do you know about that, Carli?"

"Yes. I didn't grow up with it. But since moving to the Wild Cow I've learned about it."

"And not just from book learning, right? You had your own experience?"

"Yes. We had a fire at the Wild Cow over a year ago. Lank lost a horse he had raised. We almost lost Lank and Buck. It was then that I prayed for one of the first times in my life. Lola helped me."

"I'm glad, Carli. Not for the tragedy at your ranch of course, but for what came out of that awful time. Have you ever heard of 'beauty from ashes'?"

"I think Lola has talked about that."

"It's one of my favorite verses. Isaiah 61:1-3. Part of it says, '. . . to bestow on them a crown of beauty instead of ashes, the oil of joy instead of mourning, and a garment of praise instead of a spirit of despair.' Isn't that beautiful? So, whatever happens to us, God can turn it into something good."

"Life is hard sometimes." Carli took in a big breath.

"Yes, it is. But He never promised us it would be easy. This is not heaven. Someday we'll live there.

No more pain or tears."

"Sounds great." Carli cleared her throat and blinked away tears from forming.

Karissa held out her arms and encircled Carli in a tight hug. Is this what having a mother would have felt like? Carli didn't want to let go.

"Hey, babe! You ready?" Lank and Taylor had entered the garage. "We've got to get home. Those little ruffians can't stay at Lola and Buck's all night."

Carli moved back, wiped her eye, and whispered, "Thank you. Karissa."

"Any time. You're always welcome here." Karissa held Carli's arms for an extra second.

Lank stepped forward. "Thanks much for a great dinner." He looked back at Taylor. "And a delicious steak, man." The men shook hands. "And you too, cowboy," he said to Hud, who was also standing in the garage now. "Keep up the good work and don't hurt yourself with those wild colts." Everyone chuckled.

Carli turned to Hud. "It was nice to see you, Hud. Hope you'll come to our Open House. Christmas will soon be here."

"Sure. I'll try to make it. Take care, y'all."

In the truck on the way home, Lank held her hand. "They were all nice, huh?"

"Yeah, they were." The air outside was chilly but she felt warmed from her head to her toes. She looked over at her husband. God was really good, wasn't He?

Chapter Twenty-Four

Taylor

"I think I'll check in on Shayla." Taylor put his hand on his wife's shoulder. "I'll help you clean up in a minute."

"Good idea. Let me know if she needs anything."

Tapping at her door, he called out, "Shayla, it's Dad. Can I come in?"

No answer. He knocked louder.

Finally, she answered in a soft mumble, "It's open."

She was sitting on her bed leaned against oversized pillows, earbuds fitted in her ears. Her room reflected the daughter he knew. Deep purples and bright, sunny yellows. She had begged to paint one wall of her room black, but after Karissa put her foot down, they had compromised with purple. Taylor tried to stay out of the fray, but he had to admit it looked good and fit Shayla's personality. Complicated, but always wearing a bright smile.

Her high school trophies from cheerleading competitions filled the top two shelves of a bookcase. A doll collection in the lower half. A bulletin board featured a collage of photos from various events with laughing friends. Popular and stunningly beautiful like her mother, Shayla had always been the positive force in their home, until recently. He didn't recognize the angry young woman that she was turning into, and he did not know how to relate to her. They were growing apart and he couldn't figure out how to stop it.

It was as if he had gained one daughter and was losing the other.

"Hey, sweetie. Everything okay?"

She pulled one earbud out. "Fine."

"Thanks for coming down earlier when Lank and Carli were here. Wish you could've stayed longer and joined us for dinner. I think they would have liked to have visited with you."

"What do I have to say to them? I don't know them."

"Shayla, none of us really know them. I wish you could give them a chance. I know this is hard for you."

"This has nothing to do with me. This is all about you and your stupid mistakes." She glared at him with hard eyes.

"Why are you so angry?"

"Angry?" She took a breath and pulled the other ear bud out. "For one thing, it's all you and Mom can talk about. I'm tired of hearing about Carli all the time."

"I hadn't realized that we talked about her that much. I'm just trying to wade through this, same as you. Same as your mom. I can't ignore her, Shayla. She's a part of our family now." Taylor sat on the end of her bed. At least she was talking to him.

"We never knew she existed several months ago,

and now she's like your whole world."

"That's not true. You're my world. Your brother is my world. I would do anything for the two of you. You know that. And now I have another child who needs a father. Ignoring my past will not make it go away."

"Your past has nothing to do with me." She folded her arms across her chest and avoided his eyes, looking down at the bed instead.

"That's where you're wrong, sweetheart. You have a half-sister now."

"You're going to her Open House and not to my work party. Like I said, Carli is all that you focus on now." Anger radiated from her as she glared at him.

This conversation seemed to be at a stalemate. She was being completely unreasonable. Taylor knew his anger and frustration with her might cause him to say things he would regret later. He kept his voice steady. "Shayla, we have discussed this already. Your mom and I will make every effort to be at both places. I'm not really paying Carli any more attention, sweetie. Tonight was just to be polite. To try to get to know them."

"Why? Why do we have to get to know them?" Her voice was strong.

"Because, Shayla, we found out that Carli has a connection to our family. We can't just ignore that."

"She's *not* a part of our family! Just because you had a hook-up when you were a teenager, why does that mean she can force her way into our family?"

"Sweetie, for one thing, don't be rude. And no one is forcing their way into our family. I told you at her wedding that you are my little girl. I knew you, and loved you, before you were born. When you were a pink, squalling little bundle of joy. I can still know Carli though. It doesn't mean I'm gonna love you any less."

Her head lowered.

"Shayla, I'm not asking you to be best friends with Carli. I'm just asking you not to be rude. Try being civil, polite. Let's all get along." He pinched her foot through the blanket. "Besides, Christmas is coming. You don't want to get coal in your stocking, do ya?" He tickled her foot.

She wiggled it away. "Dad, stop. Sometimes you treat me like I'm still two."

"In my mind, you are still two. That's how I will always think of you, even on the day you become a mother. A child is one of the greatest joys in the world. You'll always be my joy. I love you very much."

Her lips went to the side in a smirk, and she shrugged. "I love you too, Daddy."

"Now listen to me carefully, Shayla. Your relationship with Carli can be whatever you want it to be, however you feel comfortable." He leaned closer to her face. "Let me assure you that Carli is no mistake. The good Lord blessed me with another daughter. A child I knew nothing about. God doesn't make mistakes."

Quietly, "I'll try," came out of her mouth.

"That's all I'm asking, sweetie. Just try. I know you can do it. You're my girl."

He reached towards her for a hug. And she let him.

Chapter Twenty-Five

Carli

"Did Mom write us an email?" Zane stood at the top of the stairs.

It was the first question out of Zane's mouth when they walked into the cookhouse.

"Let's go then, and we will check."

Zane made it down the stairs in record time and dashed out into the night making a beeline towards Carli's house.

Lola, Buck, and Junior took the stairs a little more slowly.

"I think he's really missing his mother," said Lola.

"I know he is, and I'm sure Junior is too." Carli placed a reassuring hand on the boy's shoulder. "They'll be back in time for our Open House, I'm sure."

"Good night, Junior. We sure had fun. I hope you'll come back," Lola said and then turned to Carli. "How did your dinner go?"

Lank put an arm around Junior's shoulder and Carli gave Lola a quick hug. "Thanks to you both. The dinner went well. I'm glad I went."

Back at her house, Carli clicked on the computer with both boys anxiously watching the blank screen. Zane crawled up in her lap again. Time slowed down to a snail's pace as they waited. The internet service could be sluggish sometimes.

Finally. "Yes, there is a new email from Kelly." Carli clicked open. "Lank! Your sister wrote another email."

"Can I read it?" Junior asked.

"Go for it."

Dear Matt Jr., Zane, Lank, and Carli,

Hope y'all are doing well. Boys, are you being good for Aunt Carli and Uncle Lank? I hope so.

I miss you a lot. But just think, when we get back together, we can give each other BIG HUGS and kisses, too.

Dad is doing really good work at his job. We can all be proud of him.

The weather here is okay, kind of chilly, maybe in the forties. And sometimes at dusk we see that famous London fog rolling in.

And guess what? The other day one of Dad's co-workers took us to see Buckingham Palace. That's where the Queen of England lives! I'm not sure she was there. They put her flag on the roof when she's home and it wasn't out. I think she has a lot of houses.

And guess what else? We were there when they were doing the Changing of the Guard. They have LOTS of beautiful horses! All black. And the guards wear red coats and the funniest tall, black, furry hats (from bear skins!) on their heads. Other guards wear gold helmets. Maybe Aunt Carli can find a picture on the computer to show you what they look like. VERY serious dudes. They are protecting the Queen after all.

I hope one day we can bring you boys here to see all the different things. It's really educational. But FUN too!

For now, I've got to sign off.

Take care.

WE LOVE YOU WITH ALL OUR HEARTS!

Mom

Junior read slowly, stumbling on the word Buckingham.

"Read it again," Zane said as he leaned closer to the screen.

So, Junior read it through a second time, and then Carli clicked her search engine and brought up a picture of the palace and the guards with gold helmets and the black horses.

"I lit a fire," said Lank as he leaned over Carli's shoulder.

"Mom and Dad went to a palace," said Zane with all the enthusiasm and wonder a six-year-old could muster. He wiggled on Carli's lap.

"Can you print the email?" asked Junior.

"I want one too," said Zane.

"No problem." Carli obliged their request, and then turned to Lank. "I'm not sure of the time difference, but do you want to answer her email?"

"Nope. Come sit by the fire."

The boys watched the printer, grabbed their pages, and shot out of the room as though the house was on fire.

"Do they ever run down?" asked Carli.

"Apparently not." Lank laughed. "Come on. I built a fire and it's going to waste."

"Sounds good to me." Carli turned off the computer and followed him into the living room. The boys were studying the email, Zane squeezed into the chair with Brute, and Junior on the floor.

Carli sank into the couch. "Should we make them go to bed?"

Lank settled into the couch next to her and put an arm around her shoulder. She leaned closer and sighed. As she looked around the room, the scene was straight out of a Hallmark movie. Two dogs, two boys, and a fire crackling, casting light on their faces.

Family.

It wasn't anything like the family she had dreamed of being a part of her entire life. She had imagined holidays playing with cousins and long tables with grandparents, aunts, and uncles. This was much better. For the first time ever, Carli knew deep down in her soul that she was where she was supposed to be at this very moment in time.

She thought of the verse in Psalms 37:4, "Delight yourself in the Lord and he will give you the desires of your heart."

Chapter Twenty-Six

Carli

Carli rolled over and snuggled against Lank's back. Dinner at the Millers still clouded her brain with worry. To say it was awkward was an understatement. For twenty-eight years her own birth father never knew she existed. How do you make up for that lost time?

The sting of never knowing him had lessened, especially since Lank came into her life. She had learned to accept things as they were and not waste time worrying over a past she could never change. Moving forward would be the challenge.

She had dreamed of finding her birth parents her whole life, but it was a dream she never admitted to herself or spoke out loud. She grew up never knowing a blood relative. No one looked like her. No one around her had any traits that she recognized. If she let it take over, it became an obsession, a hunger to know blood family, but at an early age she accepted the fact that she walked through life alone. Then, God had truly blessed her in so many unexpected ways. Now she had a husband and a ranch family.

Sitting across from the table the night before, staring at the man who had given her life was so surreal. She never imagined that she could ever experience something like that. Taylor and Karissa seemed accepting enough. Hud was a good kid, young man really, and had a good heart.

Carli had to face the reality that her half-sister may never like her. They may never be friends, but that didn't mean she would stop trying. Carli had spent her whole life alone. She wasn't going to walk away that easily now that the Millers were becoming a part of her life.

Lank rolled over and slung an arm across her stomach. "Are you awake?"

"I am now."

"Is my coffee making?"

"No, silly. It's not. I guess you should get in there and start it. I'm getting in the shower."

Lank didn't have a comeback but rolled out of bed and shuffled to the kitchen. She smiled at the sound of the coffee grinder. He had certainly been on his best behavior. A humongous dog landed on her legs and proceeded to give her morning kisses.

"Lank! You left the bedroom door open. Down, Brute. You're not supposed to be up here."

For some unknown reason, the dog, who had bonded with the boys' dad and who supposedly only bonded with one person, had now latched himself to her. Surprisingly, their other dog Lily Jane did not seem that jealous. Maybe it was because Lily Jane had resigned herself to exist as a cowdog, and went everywhere with Lank. If he didn't take her along, she got depressed, refusing to eat or drink until he got back home again.

Carli pushed Brute off the bed and sat up. Today she'd get the entire crew back to decorating. There had to be some lights for sale somewhere in the Texas Panhandle.

"I want the headquarters glowing like an airport runway on the evening of our Open House. Some place must have lights for sale. We just have to find them."

"Yes, dear. You want to light up the Wild Cow bigger and better than ever before. I know." Lank called off several store names while he flipped the bacon.

"Yes, the boys and I went to every one of those. They were all out of stock. Where else can we go? There has to be another super decorating store in this area."

"I can't think of anywhere else, babe."

"I want to get this show on the road. We have got to finish this up."

"I can make a few phone calls," Lank suggested.

"We'll split up. Maybe with all of us looking we can locate some. The strands in the basement are so old, I don't think we can find replacement bulbs."

"Junior. Zane. Food's up if you want some," Lank called out to his nephews. There was no answer from the guest room.

"Aren't you supposed to take Junior back to the doctor for a checkup?" Lank placed bacon on a plate.

"Yes, actually I am but this round is on you since you missed the hospital excitement." Carli pointed to Lank. "The appointment is tomorrow, I think. I'll text you the time and place."

"Where are those guys? I'm not cooking two

breakfasts." Lank left the kitchen and pounded on their bedroom door. "Up and at 'em, you two."

Carli heard giggles and more yelling from Lank. He had a bark but inside her husband was mush. His phone buzzed and Carli glanced at the screen. CALL ME. From Mandy.

Carli's heart froze in her throat, and she choked on her coffee. She hated to snoop on her own husband. She should say something but didn't want to start a fight first thing this morning. And even worse, she hated the fact that she couldn't trust him.

Lank skidded past her and plopped down on the barstool. "They want to sleep longer. I guess they can have cereal later. You're my witness in case my sister asks. We provided a nutritious hot breakfast."

Carli laughed. "I've got your back."

But in the back of her mind doubt rose like a blister and she couldn't help but wonder if he had hers.

Chapter Twenty-Seven

Carli

How can my head hold all of this? Junior's got a broken arm. We should contact his parents. That huge dog in my house. My birth dad and his family. Will my half-sister ever be friendly? And the whole Christmas extravaganza. What have I gotten myself into? Wish I could just get on Beau and take a nice long ride. With Lank.

Plus, the notion to contact Lank's sister would not go away.

A knock on Carli's door ended the onslaught of spinning thoughts. At least for now.

"Angie. Hey. What a nice surprise. What are you doing here?"

"Sorry to barge in, but we haven't talked in a while."

"No, we have not. It's been like a three-ring circus around here. C'mon in."

"Just wondered what was goin' on. Christmas will be here before ya know it." The tall blonde's presence always lifted Carli's spirts.

"Don't remind me. Ugh." Carli just had so much

to think about.

"Where are those little rascals? Z and Z dudes," Angie asked.

"You can't hear them?" A video was blaring. "They're in my office watching Power Rangers or something. And don't get me any more confused with their names."

"Girl, you gotta get with the times. They're probably watching something to do with superheroes." Angie always seemed to keep up with the latest.

"I have no clue."

Just then a hairy giant of a dog came into the kitchen and slurped from his water bowl making sounds of a waterfall. When he finished, and before Carli could get a towel under his chin, he eyed Angie. Wagging his tail, he proceeded to jump up, front feet planted on her chest, slobbering all the way.

"Whoa now, boy! Get down, get down."

"Brute! Bad dog. Down!" Carli scolded.

"Brute?"

"Yes. Tiny Brute, if you can believe it. He belongs to the boys' dad," Carli said. "I had to bail him out of the kennel. They had a plumbing problem, no water."

"Gee, that's crazy. Just what you need. Something else to look after."

The boys came barreling out of the back room. "We're hungry, Aunt Carli!"

"Now just a minute. Mind your manners. We have company. Say hello to Miss Angie. Remember her? She brought that new horse for my riding school."

Like little soldiers standing side by side and in a unison, monotone, robot-like sound they said, "Hello, Miss Angie."

"Hey, boys. How are ya?"

Zane piped up. "Our mom and dad are in Your-up."

"I remember. I was here the day they left," Angie said. "Are you doin' okay?"

"Not really." Zane lowered his head. Carli thought he looked like he had just lost a pet or best friend.

"What's the problem, little man?" Angie gave the little one a serious look but winked at Carli.

Zane recited a litany of monumental crises. "Junior broke his arm. It's too cold to go riding. Aunt Carli said so. I'm bored. We have to sleep in one bed."

Angie half-smiled at Carli. "Well, that's sure a bunch of problems. You know what cowboys do when they've got a lot of problems?"

His eyes lit up. "What?"

"There's a lot cowboys do. They pray, for one thing. Like for rain. Or to keep them from harm. Another thing is they tackle their chores to keep their minds off problems. But the third thing is most important."

"What's that?" The little boy's eyes were wide-open.

"They cowboy up, silly. They don't go mopin' around cryin' about their problems. They're tough. Are you tough, Zane?"

He pumped the muscle in his little arm and pulled the shirt sleeve out of the way to show it off.

"That's nothin'. Look at mine." Junior lifted his good arm and did the same.

"There ya go." Angie nodded. "Two tough cowboys. Now do you want to help me?"

All this time Carli had been straightening the living room, picking up pillows the boys had used to make a fort. She was smiling at Angie during the whole interchange with the boys and nodded her approval.

"What do ya need help with? Can we ride?" Zane's voice was full of excitement.

"No, it's too cold like your Aunt Carli said. But I do need help with one thing. We need to name that horse I brought over. That is, if it's okay with your aunt and if he doesn't have a name already."

"Fine with me," Carli said. "He doesn't have a name yet. We've been too busy."

Angie counted with her fingers. "Okay, boys. Here's his story. He's a boy, a gelding. Might be around twelve years old."

"How 'bout Brute?" Zane fired off.

"No, dummy," Junior interjected. "That's our dog."

"Junior, please. We don't call each other names," Carli reminded.

He rolled his eyes, but said, "Sorry."

Zane kept trying. "How 'bout Max? There was a Max on our video."

Angie took on a pondering look. "Maybe. That's pretty good. But let me finish his story. His color is called Dun."

"Donnie! There's a boy at school with that name." Again, from Zane who appeared to love this game.

Angie said, "Wait. He's kind of golden in color."

"Goldie!"

Junior jumped in. "Too girly."

Angie then told them, "He's got a stripe down his back like the Spanish Conquistador horses, Barb they called them."

"Barbie!"

"He's a boy, dummy," Junior said. A look from Carli. "Sorry."

"Wait." Angie held up a finger. "One more thing. His papers say, Peppy's Chance."

"Pepper!"

"But he's gold, not gray," Angie said. "Let's think about it some more."

Carlie asked, "What about the other new horse? She needs a name too."

"Right. The sorrel. What do ya think, boys?" Angie asked.

"I know! I know!" Zane's arm was reaching for the ceiling.

Junior just smirked.

"Okay. Go for it," Angie said.

"She's red. My mom has a red ring. Ruby!" Zane rubbed imaginary dust from his hands as though he had sealed the deal.

"That's pretty good. Should we all take a vote?" Angie looked from face to face.

"So, what do we have so far? Ruby and Pepper? What do you think, Junior? Do you want to name one of them?" Carli asked.

"Max. Maybe. I don't care." Junior shrugged.

Carli studied both boys. "Zane, would you be okay naming Ruby, and your brother naming the other one Max?"

A little downcast, Zane said, "I guess so."

Carli clapped a little. "Okay, it's unanimous. Good job, guys."

"Ya know, boys, another important job is making sure the horses have feed and water. We've got to fatten them up this winter." Angie reminded.

"Miss Angie's right. Then in the spring we start training them for the riding school."

Sudden tugging at the bottom of her shirt.

"Aunt Carli."

"Yes, Zane. What is it?"

"I'm hungry. And that naming stuff worked up a powerful appetite in me."

Carli chuckled. "Oh, did it now? Powerful? You know, you guys missed the breakfast that Uncle Lank cooked. How about a PB&J for now?"

"A what?"

"Peanut butter and jelly. You know what that is, don't you? PB&J."

"Ohhhhhh. I just forgot."

Junior shook his head but no name calling this time.

Maybe they were making progress.

Chapter Twenty-Eight

Mandy

Mandy turned onto Pine Lane in Dixon keeping an eye out for any passing cars. If a neighbor recognized her, they'd tell her mother, and then there'd be a discussion, and the Sunday School class would probably start a prayer chain for her. She hated being the topic of conversation among her mom's circle of friends. The thought of a roomful of holier-than-thou do-gooders analyzing the fall of Lerlene's only daughter made her blood boil. Right after her father had died, she became her mother's only project. Mandy hated being told what to do.

Her mother wouldn't be home for at least another hour. Sunday night church ran long and Lerlene always stayed late to visit. She didn't miss a day or night if the Calvary Methodist Church doors were open.

Mandy slowed and drove past her childhood home at a crawl. The house was dark except for the front porch light that puddled in the middle of the cement porch. She parked in the alley but shut her headlights off before turning down the dirt road behind the houses. This wasn't her first rodeo. She'd been sneaking out since she was fifteen.

She eased the latch on the back gate and the neighbor's dog went nuts.

"It's me, Snuffy. Hush." The dog ceased her barking and whined instead.

Mandy got in the habit of feeding her a treat so she wouldn't sound the alarm on the nights she snuck out. She and the German Shepherd called Snuffy became fast friends. Her high school antics seemed like a lifetime ago, not just four years.

The key was still in place under the doormat on the back porch. She thought about checking the window to her old room, but there'd be no way she could lug her bulging belly inside, plus it would waste time. The door opened with a turn of the key. She eased inside and paused at the familiar smell of home. Tears stung her eyes and she tried to get a grip, but a small sob escaped her lips. Stupid pregnancy hormones.

Nothing had changed, except everything was different. She wasn't the same. Her life would never be the same. And time spent with her mother was over. The things said between them could never be taken back. Words cut deep, no matter if they are meant or not, and the wound never heals.

In the dark she found her way to her old room, daring not to risk turning on the light. Using a small pen light attached to her key chain, she dug in the bottom of her closet.

"Found it," she said aloud.

A small spotted puppy pull toy. It had been her favorite, a gift from her grandparents although she didn't remember them. They both passed before she started school. She just remembered taking this toy everywhere.

Mandy couldn't find the board books, also saved from her childhood. They had been stacked in the far back corner, with the puppy toy sitting on top. She dug on both sides of her closet, moving old shoe boxes with worn tennies and threadbare sweats and hoodies. The books were gone.

She plopped on her bed and looked around her room. What else would she need? So many memories. So many pieces of her that weren't really her anymore.

A dusty homecoming mum brittle to the touch. A tube of pink lip gloss on the bedside table. She stood and traced her fingers along the giant letter M that hung on the wall, sparkling with sequins and glitter.

It all seemed so senseless. She and her mother both lonely, but not lonely enough to forgive. She messed up. Nothing new. Thank goodness her father was dead and didn't know how bad she had screwed up this time. She was the queen of bad choices but there was one thing she could do. She was going to raise this boy to be a good man. She would make her daddy proud of his grandson, and her mother too if she gave a darn.

A passing car's headlights brought her out of the memories. She did a quick search through her dresser drawers, finding a stashed and forgotten twenty-dollar bill. Socks. Worn T-shirts. Gym shorts from junior high. Why had she ever kept those? Nothing she could use.

Her pen light shed brightness around the kitchen. On the back of the kitchen chair, in the place where it always was, hung a pink, fluffy sweater. Her mother stayed cold, and her dad used to keep turning the air conditioner down because he was hot. Mandy picked up the sweater and held it to her cheek. Vanilla. Cheap perfume from Walmart. She forgot the name of it. The sweet scent of the super hold hairspray she used. Tears clogged her throat again.

Mandy put the sweater back, hugged the pull toy close to her chest and eased through the dark to the back door. It closed with a click, and she returned the key to its hiding place.

Snuffy didn't bark this time.

"Good girl," Mandy whispered.

It wasn't until she got in her car before the emotions took over. With both hands on the steering wheel, she bent forward and sobbed until there wasn't any liquid left for tears.

Suddenly the kitchen light popped on. Mandy took a sharp intake of breath and froze. Her mom would slip into that pink sweater and start making her bedtime cup of chamomile. She couldn't see her through the sheer curtains, but Mandy knew without looking inside what her routine would be. The woman was so predictable. Boring actually. One of the reasons why Mandy chose life and excitement. She couldn't remain in that stifling place any longer. And now, no more excitement for her. The only life that mattered was the one growing inside her. He'd need everything she had and then some.

She started the engine, and with the headlights still off drove slowly to the street, turned right, and didn't turn her lights on until she was two blocks away.

Yeah, those church ladies could sure have a week's worth of analysis and Bible study over the mess poor Lerlene's daughter had made of her life. A faint tickle of moisture moved down her cheeks. "Stupid pregnancy hormones," Mandy muttered.

Chapter Twenty-Nine

Carli

A frown covered her face and with a heavy heart she pushed thoughts of that text from Mandy to her husband out of her mind. Carli focused her energy on Christmas and the upcoming Open House instead. She gave Lank a kiss on the cheek and sent him over to Lola and Buck's. He promised to spread the word about finding Christmas lights. Some store somewhere must still have them in stock. At least she prayed they would. Christmas was almost here.

There was a time in her life when this holiday was just like any another day. Actually, it was more than that. It was a day Carli dreaded more than anything, but now that she had people who cared about her, she decided to embrace this time of year. After all, it was a celebration of her Lord and Savior, a time for the world to rejoice.

This year she was on a mission. She had a new husband and a ranching family in her life to celebrate with, and a legacy of a Christmas Open House to uphold. The expectations of the community with regard to her Grandma Jean would be difficult to live up to.

This morning she had tackled more garland and then looked in every cabinet and closet of her grandparents' house in hopes of finding a stash of lights. No luck. Giving up on that she turned her attention to another important piece of the Wild Cow Ranch Christmas celebration.

The tradition involved cookies. Lots of cookies. She saw no reason to change that, but the specifics were vague. Some friends and neighbors brought a dozen or so, but from what most people told her, Grandma had baked for weeks before. The only thing Carli hadn't found were her recipes. She had been through every box in the basement and dragged most of it to where it was now stacked in the garage. She had cleaned out the kitchen cabinets, drawers, and pantry. No recipe card file anywhere. Might as well rely on the professionals. Lola could do most of the baking, and she would call Belinda at the B & R Beanery to cater. They were all set, except for lights.

Rubbing the sleep from his eyes, Zane appeared at the kitchen doorway, one sock on and one bare foot. "I'm hungry. Will my mom be back today?"

Glancing at her watch, Carli gasped. "Good grief, it's almost lunch time. There are a few pieces of bacon left. Or do you want cereal?"

"Cereal, please."

Conversations with her nephews had quickly boiled down to a few key phrases relating to food. Their parents' return. Checking for emails. And, a new request for her, Carli had never said "brush your teeth" more times in her life before this week. Food seemed to be the reigning topic on a young boy's mind. These guys were never full. Despite her aggravations, Carli smiled. They were good boys. Lank's sister had taught them to have nice manners. And speaking of Kelly, they needed to tell her about Junior.

"Can I watch a video?"

Normally, she wouldn't allow milk and cereal on the living room rug, but she knew that Zane was getting homesick. As the youngest, he definitely was a mama's boy.

"Sure. But be careful, and make Brute behave. He can't drink from your bowl." For good measure, she turned to the dog. "Go to your blanket."

The dog padded across the kitchen and sprawled in the dining room on an old blanket. They really needed to go to Kelly's house and get more dog food. What the kennel had given them was running out. Also, his bed and toys. Looked like he wasn't leaving any time soon.

Carli peeked into the guest room and saw that Junior was still snuggled under the blanket. "Do you want to eat cereal with your brother?" she asked.

"No," came the muffled reply.

"Are you okay?" She walked closer, just to get a look at his face.

"My arm hurts. When will Mom get home?"

His cheeks were flushed. She felt his forehead, although she had no idea why. It was something she'd always seen mothers do. He felt unusually warm. She pulled out her phone. "Lola. Can you come over? Junior's not well."

"I'll make you some toast." While she waited for Lola to arrive, Carli kept busy and placed a buttery piece of toast on a plate. On second thought, grape jelly might be food too.

A rapid knock on the door, and Lola rushed in bringing the cold with her. "What's wrong?"

"He feels warm to me. Says his arm hurts."

"Oh no." Lola hurried to the guest room. "What are we going to do with you, Junior? Why does your arm hurt? Did you sleep wrong?"

"No."

"You do feel a little warm. Let's give him something for pain and knock that fever down. You probably should call the doctor." She turned to Carli.

"He's got a checkup tomorrow."

"I'd take him in today. Better safe than sorry."

Junior didn't want the toast, but Zane did. Carli called the doctor's office and set up an appointment for the afternoon. So much for baking and decorations. While she was in Amarillo, she'd bring something home for dinner. Kill two birds and all that.

Living in Georgia, she had rarely cooked. There were so many food places, and she saved her leftovers which got her through another day. Now, in the middle of nowhere with a small town the only resource, she had become more self-sufficient. Particularly with two kids, she had to change her way of thinking. She soon realized that any sustenance was on her. Lank was solely centered around the livestock and their needs, not two growing boys.

She texted Lank to tell him where she'd be, bundled Zane over to Lola's, and then froze in the hallway. What to do with a Bernese Mountain dog by the name of Tiny Brute? Why, send him with Lily Jane and Lank, of course. No reason this dog couldn't learn a little ranch work.

She texted Lank again.

COME GET BRUTE.

Lank texted back.

COME OUTSIDE.

Curious as to what he might be up to, she did not hesitate and grabbed a jacket from the entry hall and walked out onto the front porch. Sitting in the middle of her yard was the most beautiful wagon she had ever seen. Buck and Lank were hanging greenery along the sides.

She ran out into the yard. "I love it," she blurted. "Where did you get it from?"

"Neighbor up the road," answered Buck. "He keeps it in a shed. He used to have a pair of mules, but they're buried at the back of his pasture, and he hasn't gotten this wagon out since. I thought we might put it to good use for a few weeks."

Carli ran her hand along the smooth wood. "I'm glad you remembered it. This is perfect. We need a stuffed cowboy Santa to sit on the seat. Maybe I can find a Santa suit somewhere."

"I'll put a few bales of hay in the back. Colton knows a guy who has a mule team. Maybe we can offer rides."

"That would be so much fun." Carli clapped her hands. This was coming together just like she'd hoped.

Chapter Thirty

Hi Boys!

(and Aunt Carli and Uncle Lank, too! LOL.)

Hope everyone is doing fine. I can't wait to hear all the exciting things you boys are doing. Are you helping your Aunt and Uncle around the ranch? I sure do hope so.

Christmas is coming! Are you helping decorate the Wild Cow? We can't wait to see how pretty it will look. And remember, Santa knows where to find all of us.

Most days when your Dad is working, I explore on my own. We go together on the weekend or sometimes late in the afternoon if he can get off work early.

The other day we got to tour Westminster Abbey. It's a VERY OLD church, more than 1,000 years old, and it's REALLY BIG! A lot of famous people are buried there like: Sir Isaac Newton. He was a scientist. Geoffrey Chaucer, a poet. Queen Elizabeth the first. William Wilberforce. He fought against slavery. Since you're out of school now, con-

sider this a little history lesson.

I'm going to find out about my cellphone so that I can call you. If it takes a while to figure out, maybe I can call from Daddy's office or from the hotel.

In the meantime, please be good boys. And help your Aunt and Uncle.

WE LOVE YOU WITH ALL OUR HEARTS!

Mom

Chapter Thirty-One

Carli

Carli met Lank at the front door and planted a kiss on his lips, a bit cool from being outside.

"What was that for?" he said before pulling her close for another.

"Two reasons. One, I hung some mistletoe over the doorway." They both looked up and he grinned. His lips brushed against hers again, but she kept talking. "And two, I really love the wagon sitting in my front yard. Thank you."

"Gross!" declared Zane as he ran past them inside the house.

"And there's more." She pushed him away.

"Oh, no. You trapped me," he said.

"Lank. You *have* to tell your sister." Carli studied her husband to make sure he was listening. They hadn't heard much from the boys' parents, other than a few emails and that had her worried.

"I will."

"Today."

"Okay. I will try to get through. I hate to text her about it."

"If I were a mom, I'd want to know that my child broke his arm."

"She might freak," he said.

"I don't even know how to begin to explain what happened. She's your sister, so will you call her?"

"I hope she doesn't hop on a plane and try to get home."

He did have a good point. "Just reassure her that Junior is doing fine. There's nothing to worry about."

The boys were laughing and shouting from the bedroom.

"Junior must be feeling better. The boys are playing together again." Carli smiled.

"Stop it!"

"You stop it!"

"That doesn't sound like playing." Lank left the room. Carli followed close behind but before they got there they heard a scream.

"Owwww!"

Tiny Brute went crazy with his barking. Lank and Carli stepped into the chaos.

Junior stood on the bed looking down at Zane who held his arm, tears streaming down his cheeks.

"He fell off the bed," said Junior above the dog's barking. And of course, since Brute was carrying on, Lily Jane had to add her two cents.

"You guys know not to jump on the bed," said Carli.

She kneeled next to Zane, but Lank already had him sitting up.

"Where does it hurt?" asked Lank.

"I think I need a rolled-up magazine," Zane stuttered as tears streamed down his cheeks.

Carli stifled a laugh because it was so bizarre and

so horrible, it wouldn't do to burst into tears either.

"Let's get you to the emergency room," said Lank as he lifted Zane.

"Come on, Junior. Let's go," said Carli.

"I broke mine first," he said with pride.

"This isn't a contest, you guys. This is very serious. If we don't return you in one piece, your parents will never let you stay here again."

Silently they filed out to the pickup truck after grabbing coats and hats. Carli helped Zane keep his coat on over his shoulders. With every little bump Lank hit in the road, Zane muttered a soft, "Ow."

Carli felt like bursting into tears. "Are boys usually this rowdy?"

"Yes. Always. Plus, it's too cold to go outside, and they've been cooped up because of the weather. They're missing the stuff in their room."

"Oh, that reminds me. We should pick up more dog food at your sister's house, and I guess the boys can get whatever they want."

Lank's phone buzzed. "Hello?" He looked at the screen.

"Mandy. Hi." He cast a glance at Carli.

"No, sorry. Not this afternoon. I'm taking my nephew to the hospital."

Carli could not believe this girl. The blatant, outright disregard for a man's family. Surely she had family in town that could help her. And coworkers. There were lots of people employed at the sale barn. They should be helping their own, and she should not be calling Lank. It just wasn't proper.

Lank listened for a few more minutes without response, and then ended the call. Silence in the pickup cab hung like a gray shroud. Carli was not going to ask what the girl wanted, and apparently Lank was not going to tell her. Fine. She would wait him out. That lasted a few more miles.

"What did she want?" asked Carli, keeping her voice steady and kind, although that did not reflect the turmoil that raged inside.

"Her old car again."

"Doesn't she have anyone else she can call?"

"No." And that was the end of that conversation.

They rode in silence and Carli considered her options regarding Mandy. Nagging Lank about her would not fix the problem. He was a good guy, and she knew that he would do anything for anybody, male or female. But did it have to be an ex-girlfriend?

They pulled to a stop under the portico, and the emergency room nurse met them at the sliding doors with a wheelchair.

"You people look familiar," she said with a laugh.

"Can you believe we may have another broken arm?"

"No kidding?" For a minute she hesitated, as though they were making a joke and then she saw Zane's tear-streaked, ashen face. The nurse became all business. Within minutes they were all hustled inside, and Zane was on his way for x-rays.

"I bet mine hurt worse than his," said Junior.

"No more competition," said Lank. "This is horrible. How can I ever explain this to your mom?"

He'd better not chicken out again. Carli glanced at her husband; his face was as ashen as his nephew's.

An attendant ushered them to an exam cubicle with a hospital bed in the emergency department. Several of the nurses said hello to Junior and asked how his arm was doing.

Zane returned to them from x-rays riding in a wheelchair with a warm, creamy white blanket over his lap and a lollipop in his mouth.

"I didn't get one of those," said Junior. The nurse pulled another from his pocket and handed it to him with a smile.

"Thank you."

There was nothing Carli or Lank could do to calm down Zane, whose mood changed minute by minute. He wanted his mother. That was clear. After more waiting while Zane softly sobbed, the doctor finally came into their room.

"He's being a baby," said Junior.

"I am not!" shouted Zane.

"I can't even imagine how bad it hurts to break a bone. Both of you are very brave," said Carli.

It was a break for sure, as they all could see on the film.

"Looks clean," the doctor said. "It's really nothing serious as far as bone injuries go. I don't think we'll need to do surgery. I have scheduled an OR to set the cast, so if you folks can hang out here, we will get him in as soon as we can. I have to ask how this happened." He looked at Lank. "Two boys with broken arms."

Lank stood. "I'm their uncle. Their parents are in Europe. This one accidently toppled off a ladder while helping us hang decorations." He pointed to Junior, then Zane. "And this one accidently fell off a bed. I'm not sure what was going on. My wife and I were in another room."

"That's the story we got too. Apparently, the game on the bed was King of the Mountain." The doctor chuckled.

Lank cut an angry glare at both boys. "Thank you, Doctor." After the doctor left, he said, "There's no other king but me, and you guys need to be more careful. This is getting ridiculous. How am I ever going to explain this to your parents?"

"Well, while you ponder how you're going to tell your sister," Carli said, "I'm going to take Junior over to his doctor's appointment. We'll be back as soon as we can."

If it weren't so serious, it would be funny. Carli knew that Lank really looked up to his older sister, Kelly. And now he was going to have to tell her that both her boys had broken arms. She was totally at a loss as to how they should approach this problem. Text, telephone, an email? Either option was going to result in a response that they could not judge from halfway around the world.

As soon as she got back to the exam room, she brought the topic up again.

"Now will you call your sister?" Carli raised an eyebrow at Lank. He stared straight ahead, never glancing in her direction.

"I think I'll write a letter," he said.

"Can we write Mom a letter, too?" both boys asked at once.

"I don't think it will reach her before they get home," said Carli.

Lank plopped into a straight-back chair, stretched his long legs out in front, and crossed his arms over his chest. "Exactly."

Chapter Thirty-Two

Carli

Carli wished she could get on Beau and ride for a few hours. Alone.

Away from little boys, although cute as could be, who roughhoused and broke their bones. Even away from Lank, as much as she loved him with her whole heart, who stayed in contact with his old girlfriend. Away from the stress of putting together an Open House for the town, one that her grandparents, if they were alive, would be proud of.

"Santa was here!" Zane screamed at the side of her face.

Dear Lord. She rubbed her ear.

"What are you talking about?"

"The packages! Look at your porch. All those boxes. Maybe it's from Mom and Daddy!"

They were just returning from their second trip to the hospital with a different nephew now sporting a broken arm—this time Zane, the youngest. It didn't seem to slow him down much.

Lank, who was driving their truck, looked over at Carli. "What do you think all of that is for? And who sent it? Must've been delivered by mistake."

"I have no idea." Carli mentally counted the boxes on her porch. At least ten. Maybe the counting could also help her regain some calmness. Maybe.

"No mistake!" Zane announced from the backseat with his brother. "Santa don't make mistakes."

"Doesn't," Carli said.

"That's what I said," Zane countered.

When Lank cut off the motor, Carli held up a finger and said, in as calm a voice as she could muster, "When I open this door, I do not want you boys to run. I do not want you to touch those boxes. Do you understand me?"

A low mutter from Lank. "Good luck with that."

"Yes, Aunt Carli," the boys replied in unison.

She waited a second, got out of the vehicle, and then opened the back door to the super cab. They spilled out almost at the same time. Once on the ground, Zane looked at Junior. "First one to the boxes!"

"No, Zane. Aunt Carli said not to," Junior said.

Older brother responsibility must sometimes be a burden, Carli thought. She pictured him as an adult, like his dad.

But it was too late. Zane was already zooming to the porch examining the mysterious treasure trove.

"Hey! These boxes are already half-open. And they're not wrapped like presents. No name tags." He was ready to dig in, but Carli stopped him.

"Just wait, Zane. They may not be for us."

Junior held up a piece of paper. "Here's a note. It was taped to one of the boxes."

Carli read it. "We heard you were low on lights. Hope these help. You can keep them. We always loved the Christmas display your grandparents put on. Thanks for carrying on the tradition."

She opened the folded box lid to see the lights inside were multi-colored M&M figures with white shoes, white gloves, and smiley faces. "Be careful with these," she said to Zane who nosed around everything. "They could break."

"Look at this one," Lank said. "Deer."

Zane ran to that box. "Wow! We can blow them up!"

"Inflatables," Junior said. He read the outside of the box: "Three-Piece Lighted Holiday Deer Family."

Box after box held assorted lights. Some had black and white cow figures dotting the wire. There was one with golden stars of Bethlehem attached. Another box contained pink lights in the shape of breast cancer ribbons. Not exactly Christmassy, Carli thought, but would add to the rainbow of colors that was growing.

Other boxes held loose decorations, not lights. Candy canes, mittens, stockings, gingerbread men. A separate box was crammed with red, velvety bows.

Kind of a mish mosh, Carli thought, but all were sent with love.

"What's this say?" Zane inspected a large box.

Junior read the side. "Laser Decorative Christmas Light Projector."

"Cool! We can beam pictures on the wall." Zane was about to bust.

"What are we going to do with all this stuff?" Carli asked Lank.

"I guess decorate, decorate, decorate. That's what you wanted to do, right?" He put an arm around her.

"That's what I want you and Buck to do." She

winked.

Lola came across the yard. "Oh, good, you're all home. How's the latest patient?" She reached down to hug Zane.

"See my cast, Aunt Lola?" The little boy held his plastered arm up high.

"Yes, it's mighty fine. Just promise us not to break anything else, okay?"

"I'll try," he said.

Lola came closer to Lank and Carli. "I see the townsfolk have been donating decorations. Isn't it wonderful?"

"I guess you made some calls?" Carli grinned.

"Well, to a few church ladies. You know how fast news travels in a small town." Lola's face was the picture of an innocent angel.

"Okay, boys, you can pull everything out and let's see what we've got."

Big smiles covered their faces as they began lifting strands of lights out of the boxes and bags.

"Stretch them out on the lawn," said Lank.

Each different strand brought a comment or "Look at this one" from Zane or Junior. Sometimes they would stop their own work to admire what the other held in his hand. Before long, the front yard was an eclectic mix of shapes and colors, all waiting to be hung and plugged in.

Before long, Buck wandered over and watched their progress.

"Where should we start?" asked Lank. "I guess it doesn't matter because not one of them is the same as the other. What do you think, Buck? Where did you string lights in years past?"

Buck rubbed his gloves together. It was cold.

"The top rail of the fences that line both sides of the roadway leading to headquarters, but we used all white. This will make an interesting display. That's for sure."

"Sounds great to me. I'll go get the extension cords."

The boys had left a pile of empty sacks and containers on her front porch. They both sat on the front steps and looked at her with big, sorrowful eyes. Before they could speak, Carli said, "Let me guess. You're hungry now."

They nodded their heads.

Lola laughed. "I can fix that. When y'all are done, come over and I'll have something ready."

"I want a hot chocolate," said Zane.

"With marshmallows, I'm assuming. No problem," said Lola.

Relief washed over Carli as the only thing she could think of for hungry boys was mac and cheese. If she never saw another plate of mac and cheese again in her life, she could die a contented woman.

"Thanks, Lola." Carli waved after her and then turned back to the boys. "If we all work together, we can get done faster. How about it?"

Reluctantly they stood and using their good hands, began dragging strands out to the road where Lank and Buck were already working.

It was going to look fabulous, even with chili peppers and golden orbs and bright white snowflakes. Who says Christmas has to be coordinated?

Chapter Thirty-Three

Dear Boys, and Carli and Lank,

I hope you know that in different countries around the world people might talk different than we do in Texas. Even in different states of our own country, people might talk different. In London we've had to learn different expressions. And remember, we can't laugh at other people even if it might sound funny to us. We wouldn't want them to laugh at our expressions, would we? Here goes:

Money – one pound equals about $1.35. The subway here is called The Tube. Loo is the toilet. Cheers is not just to toast with a drink, but also to say thanks. Mate is a friend. Cheerio is not a cereal, but means "see you later." Jim jams are pajamas (my favorite!). Bangers and mash are sausages and mashed potatoes. Fish and chips – that's battered, fried fish. The chips are actually like French fries. In the old days, Londoners ate their fish and chips on newspaper because it saved money on plates and the food was greasy. Can you imagine eating on newspaper at home? I'd be afraid the ink on the *paper would come off on my fish and then I'd eat the ink too. Yuck. But nowadays they use better grease-proof paper that just looks like newspaper. The fish was good!*

That's fun, isn't it? Now remember to wear your jim jams to bed! Cheerio for now, mateys! LOL.

Hope you're being good boys and helping around the ranch.

WE LOVE YOU WITH ALL OUR HEARTS! (and miss you!)

Mom

Chapter Thirty-Four

Mandy

Bawling cattle, clanking gates, and a cowboy's shouts distracted Mandy's efforts at adding up the invoice in front of her on the gritty counter. It was all she could do not to scream her head off. Her back hurt like crazy when she woke from that stupid cot and it still hadn't eased off, plus little man kept pressing on her bladder. She couldn't get any work done traipsing back and forth to the restroom.

"One more time," she muttered to herself. She punched keys as the adding machine tape rolled out with a click, click, click. And . . . wrong again. She now had three different totals for the same column of numbers. Great. It was going to be one of those days.

"Let me try that again. One sec." She gave him a friendly smile.

The rancher standing at the counter waiting to pay was not amused as he watched her. After several more attempts, she finally got the same answer twice, completed the paperwork, and then ran the man's card through the machine.

"Thank you for joining us today," she said. "Be back in one sec."

Candace nodded her head and Mandy waddled at a fast pace towards the hallway. She had been sitting at the desk way too long this time. Little man demanded the frequent bathroom trips. As she rounded the corner, she bumped into a solid wall of cowboy who smelled of musk cologne. Not like the bodies that normally hung around the sale barn, sweat with a slight tinge of manure.

"Excuse me, sir," she said as she flew past him, her eyes focused on the ladies' room door.

"Mandy. It's me."

She paused for one second and looked up into the face of Phineas Shelton who didn't look anything like a farmer this morning. Without response she disappeared into the restroom. After she washed her hands, she leaned over the sink and took several deep breaths. What was he doing here again? She glanced in the mirror and was surprised that her hair looked halfway decent this morning. She had put on makeup and wore a new shirt that her boss's wife had given her. Bright red with a bow tie at the waist, it was a maternity blouse instead of the oversized T-shirts she usually stretched over her belly. She felt kind of pretty, and more like herself instead of bigger than a load of hay. Following a quick swipe of stardust shimmer pink on her lips, she walked back into the hall. He was still there.

"Can I buy you lunch?" He tipped his hat, and one corner of his mouth went up into a half-smile.

She surveyed Phineas Shelton from head to toe, except it wasn't the same man from several weeks ago. Instead of a ball cap and well-worn overalls, he stood before her in starched jeans, boots, and a paisley pearl snap shirt. The impressive buckle on his flat middle read BRONC RIDING CHAMPION, and his black felt hat seemed to tower over his head. He looked handsome. In fact, he looked so darn good she couldn't take her eyes off him.

"You clean up real nice." That came out before she could stop it. Her mouth had no filter and usually got her into trouble.

"Thank ya." He didn't wipe the grin off his face.

They both stared at each other for an awkward silence.

"Mandy!" Calvin stuck his head around the corner. "There you are."

"On my way, boss."

Phin put his hand on her arm. "What about lunch?"

If she hadn't been so hungry, she would have immediately told him in no uncertain words to get lost, but there he was all shiny and polite. She couldn't bring herself to reject him.

"I guess, but it'll be late after the sale."

"I'll wait," he said.

The morning went by in a dizzying rush of buyers and numbers and delivery addresses. She emerged from the office, stretched her back, and noticed Phin standing in the hallway. She had forgotten about him and then she forgot where she was going.

"Are you hungry?" he asked.

"Starving."

"Do you want to go somewhere, or do you want to eat here?"

"Here is fine. I really like their cheeseburgers."

He chuckled. "Me too. I was hoping you'd want to stay."

"I'll be back in a few minutes."

"I can order for us and get a table."

She nodded her head in agreement and they parted, going in opposite directions. What was she doing? What was he doing here? She couldn't get in the habit of eating lunch with their customers. For one thing, she was nine months pregnant. People would talk more than they had been about her. For two, he was a client of the sale barn. And for three, she could deliver at any minute! What in the world was he thinking asking her to lunch?

With a sigh, she finished up a few things in the office and then remembered she needed to deliver a message to one of the yard guys from his wife. So, she went out the front door and walked around until she got the cowboy's attention. He steered his horse over to her. With that done, she walked back inside and headed to the dining area.

Phin sat at a back table, food arranged neatly in front of him. She sank into the chair opposite and took a minute to inhale the aroma of burger, crisp tater tots, and he had even gotten her a bowl of hot peach cobbler. She glanced up into the most beautiful blue eyes she had ever seen. Eyes that studied her intently.

"Thank you for all of this," she said. "Mr. Shelton."

"You're welcome. Thank you for joining me. I'd really like it if you called me Phin."

She picked up her burger and opened her mouth wide, then nodded in answer.

"Do you mind if we bless the food first?"

Heat warmed her cheeks as she set her burger

back down. She bowed her head and clasped her hands on the table.

"Thank you for this day, Lord. May everyone be safe, both animal and man. Bless this food. Amen."

"Amen," she muttered.

"How is your morning going, Mandy?" He asked before he took a bite.

"Busy. It's a sale day." She stated the obvious and then thought how stupid that sounded.

He chuckled. She focused on her food.

"What are you doing here? You didn't buy anything at the sale," she finally asked as she pushed aside the paper wrapper and pulled the dessert closer. She picked up her spoon and paused, giving him a curious glance.

"I came here to see you," he said. "Is there anything you need?"

She hesitated before she answered. Her car wasn't acting right, and she had another doctor's appointment. She had texted Lank yesterday and had even called him because she was desperate. He had been busy with his nephews.

During the final weeks of her pregnancy, the doctor had her scheduled to come every week, and she could not miss. The more knowledge she had of the process, the more comfortable she felt. Talking to the doctor and nurse eased her nerves. They understood what she was going through. This was something she had to face alone.

She studied Phin's friendly face for a few minutes.

"Actually, there is one favor. You can say no, if it's not something you want to do."

"Go on," he said.

"I need a ride to my doctor's office. Tomorrow afternoon. I'm not sure that my car will make it."

"Consider it done. Mandy." He stood to clear their table. She stood and followed him to the trash.

"Thanks, Phin. That was very good."

He tipped his hat. "Thanks for having lunch with me. I'll be here tomorrow to pick you up. I think you have my cell phone in the file. Just text me the time and place."

She watched him stride towards the exit, broad shouldered, tall and straight. What was he thinking, spending time with her? He must be stupider than he looked.

Chapter Thirty-Five

Mandy

The first thing Mandy did was find Mr. Shelton's information and text him the time of her appointment and the address of her doctor. They'd need to leave about one hour early from the sale barn to drive to the next town over. Calvin had already given his okay for her to take off the rest of the day.

The morning seemed to crawl by. She forced herself to focus on the paperwork, but finally gave in and dragged out the vacuum. If she couldn't focus on numbers, she could at least clean. After noon, she tidied up her desk and checked to make sure her blouse was dry. She had rinsed the dust out from yesterday and hung it in the storeroom over the cot and then managed to shower at the truckstop later that evening. She didn't have any other nice shoes except for boots. They'd have to do. Dry shampoo did wonders with her hair, and she carefully applied makeup. It was only the doctor. He'd seen her at the very worst before. But her heart thudded.

With a few minutes to spare, Mandy eased onto

the bench in front of the sale barn. Even with a chill in the air, the sun's heat radiated directly on the entrance area. She closed her eyes and focused on the warmth that covered her bare skin. Tires crunched gravel and she opened her eyes to see Phin pulling to a stop right in front of her. He hopped out and offered a hand to help her up from the bench. Easier said than done. As he tugged at her hand his fingers were strong and warm.

"Let's get you in the truck," he said. Those blue eyes again that bore a hole straight to her soul.

"You're lifting two, ya know," she said with a giggle. He looked punchy again today, with starched jeans instead of overalls.

"It's not a problem. I have a strong back." And then he blushed after he said that.

Mandy stifled another giggle. Settled in the seat, he had to help her stretch the seat belt over that much belly. She blushed.

"How much longer before we get to meet the little guy?" Phin asked.

"I think a few weeks to go, but I may have lost track. And the doctor says you can never tell with the first one. He keeps growing and I keep gaining weight. I don't know if my stomach will stretch any more." She regretted that the minute it slipped from her lips. "I'm sorry. That was probably more information than you wanted to know."

"I want you to feel comfortable around me, Mandy, and say whatever you want. I don't judge others. That's God's job."

He may talk a good talk, but all men were alike. They knew just the right things to say to make you believe their motives were sincere. Just smoke and mirrors, most of them.

They rode in silence, but Mandy wasn't worried about trying to make small talk. Phin was the most easygoing, confident man she'd ever been around. He didn't force a conversation and neither did she. The sense of peace and safety that came over her as he drove astonished her.

"Is this the right place?"

"Yes. I go through that door there." She pointed.

He parked, hopped out, and was standing at the opened door before she could even swing her leg around. She accepted the hand he offered.

"I'll be right here waiting."

"Would you like to come in and see the baby on the sonogram?" Regret hit her the minute that question escaped her lips, but she couldn't take it back.

Surprise reflected in his eyes and a broad smile spread across his face. "I would. Thank you."

He followed her inside, she checked in with the receptionist, and they waited about fifteen minutes before she was called back to an exam room. She stretched out on the exam table and the nurse raised her shirt. Phin turned and faced a corner, which made her laugh.

"After that roll in the bar ditch, I think you've seen just about everything."

The nurse looked at her questioningly, and so they had to relate the story with everyone in a fit of giggles by the time the doctor came in. He asked what was so funny, so they had to tell it again.

The doctor spread gel on the wand and they all anxiously watched the monitor. And there he was. A little hand held up in front of the outline of a little face. Forehead, button nose, and a strong chin. The hand drifted closer. It looked like he was sucking his thumb. Mandy couldn't believe it.

Phin stared intently, his eyes never blinking, and he never looked away. "He sure is sumthin'," he muttered.

She had never shared this moment with anyone other than the clinic staff, and emotion bubbled to the surface bringing tears to her eyes. Phin looked at her, his eyes wide with wonder, and they exchanged knowing smiles as a warm glow flowed through her.

"Everything looks good. It could be any day now." The doctor wiped the gel from her belly and pulled her shirt down. "You call me, if you have any pain at all."

"I will," she assured him.

He wrote a prescription to refill her prenatal vitamins. They were terribly expensive, more than an entire week's wages. The doctor had delivered Mandy, and he knew her situation which was why he had agreed to take on her case for free. She could never repay him for the kindness he had shown.

Phin said, "I'll be in the waiting room."

After the doctor and Phin left, the nurse returned to help finish wiping off her stomach. She also carried sample boxes of the vitamins which Mandy stuffed in her purse. If she spread them out over several weeks by taking one every other day, they might last. She had been consciously drinking a lot of milk with her meals too, instead of sodas.

The nurse opened a cabinet door and pulled out a bright blue diaper bag. Mandy took it from her and looked inside. There were more samples of diapers, burp pads, onesies, powder, and diaper cream. The bag was stuffed full of items.

"I can't accept this," Mandy said. They were already doing so much for her.

"We give one of these to all of our new mothers. It's okay. The companies provide the samples for our patients. We'll see you next week."

In the waiting room, Phin opened the door for her, and they walked back outside towards his truck.

"Are you hungry?"

She glanced at him but didn't answer.

"That was a stupid question." They both laughed. "Let me try again. Would you like to go somewhere for dinner? What sounds good?"

Anything and everything sounded good, but she hated to answer the question specifically. She hadn't had a good meal in . . . well, she couldn't even recall when she'd had a good meal. Probably at home cooked by her mother was the last time, and that had been right after high school.

"Anything but really spicy foods. This little guy gives me lots of trouble if I eat anything like that."

"I'm hungry for a good steak," he said, "If that sounds okay to you."

Moments later, they were seated at a table in the corner of a local steak joint surrounded by a few deer heads, original western art, and country music softly playing overhead. Mandy took a sip of her sweet tea and glanced up to see Phin staring, his eyes keen and assessing.

"Are you feeling all right?" he asked.

"Fine." She took another swallow.

"That was amazing. I've never seen anything like that."

Emotion overwhelmed her from the look on his face and the sincere comment. This man didn't seem to have a hidden agenda. What you saw was what you got.

"I know," was the only answer she could come up with. The entire process of producing another human being was overwhelming.

By the time their food arrived, they had slipped into an easy conversation about the auction barn and what it took behind the scenes to make everything run. Mandy loved talking about her job. Phin told her more about his ranch and farm. He raised Red Angus cattle and trained horses in his spare time. He seemed to be a master at a lot of things.

For dessert they shared apple cobbler with ice cream. She was growing used to looking into those blue eyes.

"How old are you?" she asked.

"Twenty-six."

He was younger than he looked. "Ever been married?"

"No."

"Got any kids you know of?"

"I don't have any kids. That I'm sure of."

"Always lived with your parents?"

"I've always lived and worked on my family's place, if that's what you mean. I did leave and go to college for two years but hated every minute of it."

"Why are you here with me? Don't you got something better to do?"

His blue eyes were gentle and contemplative, and then turned to a gleam of interest. "I thought you might need a friend."

"I'm not some charity case. I can take care of myself. What do you want from me?" It stung her heart to ask the question, but there was always a catch. People weren't just nice for no reason.

"It's not anything like that, Mandy. I like you. I want to get to know you better."

"Why me?" she asked.

"Why not you?" he replied. "You're smart. I like talking to you. And you're the most beautiful girl I've ever known."

There it was. That line of BS that all guys eventually reveal. They can't help it. But when she looked into those blue eyes, she saw only sincerity and a spark of interest. Could this guy be for real?

"Thanks for the ride and thanks for the dinner. I need to get back to the sale barn now."

Without any further conversation, he paid their check, and helped her into the pickup truck. They drove in silence through the Texas Panhandle back to the next little town where he parked beside her car.

"Good night and thanks again. I really appreciate it, Phin."

After he helped her out, he waited in his truck while she pretended to fumble with her car keys. She turned and waved but he kept sitting there.

"Is there a problem?" she walked up to his window.

"Just making sure you get home all right. I hope your car starts."

"Ya know what, I just remembered that I should probably go check emails since I've been gone all afternoon. So, you can go ahead and leave because

I'll be working a little bit longer. Thanks again. See you around, Phin."

The look on his face told her he didn't quite believe what she was telling him, but he drove away. Mandy collapsed on the bench and watched his taillights until she couldn't see them anymore. She had no idea why tears were streaming down her cheeks.

Chapter Thirty-Six

Dear Boys, and Lank and Carli,

There are LOTS of museums in London! The British Museum was free. One Saturday we spent a few hours going through it. Tons of Egyptian sculptures. You would have liked the mummies! (not mommies! LOL) There was pottery from Greece; they said it was as old as 1000 BC. Do you know what that means? Before Christ. Wow. They had art and artifacts—that means "old stuff"—and something from almost every country in the world! China, Japan, Africa, India, the Middle East. Maybe Aunt Carli or Uncle Lank can show you the museum's website. It was an amazing place. There's so much to learn about the world. I hope one day you boys will travel. Like explorers!

WE LOVE YOU WITH ALL OUR HEARTS! (and miss you!)

Mom

Chapter Thirty-Seven

Dear Boys, and Lank and Carli,

We went to the Tower of London. It was used as a prison and in the old days, bad guys were executed there. Yikes! On a happier note, we saw the crown jewels. Rubies, emeralds, diamonds! I wish I could have tried one of the crowns on. LOL. But there was an armed guard protecting them! Some jewels had a sign saying they were "in use" so I guess the Queen had a special party to go to. LOL.

And out on the lawn were the famous ravens. They're like big crows. They sure did squawk a lot. Some of their names were: Jubilee, Rocky, Erin, Poppy, and Georgie. There's a "Ravenmaster" in charge of the birds. The birds eat meat, biscuits, and blood. (Yuck!) But the public is not supposed to feed them. You'd get in BIG trouble if you did!

There are a lot of legends about the birds. Some say ravens first came to the Tower around the 1600s. Or maybe one of the kings brought them there. I forget what the tour guide said. Legends say

the modern ravens are descendants of those first birds. What do you think, boys?
 WE LOVE YOU WITH ALL OUR HEARTS! (and miss you!)
 Mom

Chapter Thirty-Eight

Dear Junior, Zane, and Lank and Carli,
The London Eye – this is a giant Ferris wheel.
We decided we're not going on it until you boys can
come with us. It's 400 feet high! Would you want to
ride on it? It's not fast. It takes about thirty minutes
and goes real slow so you can see amazing views of
the whole city.
WE LOVE YOU WITH ALL OUR HEARTS!
(and miss you!)
Mom

Chapter Thirty-Nine

Carli

"That's it, boys. You are caught up with your mom's emails. Y'all can go play now, unless you have schoolwork to do."

They sounded like a herd of elephants as boots scrambled out of her office to the living room where they proceeded to argue over the television remote. Carli clicked her computer off and thought about what was next on the agenda. What she'd really like to do is sit in the quiet with her husband.

People joke about the honeymoon being over. Gosh, she hoped hers wasn't. But they didn't even go on a honeymoon. Maybe that was the problem? They just jumped right back into their crazy life. Wait. She loved her life on the ranch. She loved her husband. However, it seemed the universe was conspiring to throw stuff at her. Life challenges, Lola would call them.

Guilt stung her every time she looked at her nephews. Of course, the new in-law would take most of the blame. Kelly and Matt would never forgive them. The more she nagged Lank, the more he resisted but she couldn't help it. She heard him in the kitchen.

"Lank. You have *got* to call your sister. She needs to know about her kids."

"I tried." He wandered into her office.

"Well, what happened? Did you leave a message?"

"It made a funny noise and didn't go through."

"Did you try again?"

"A couple times."

"Did you try Matt's work? They left us with a number."

"I didn't want to bother him."

"You're kidding."

"No. What do ya mean?"

Carli drew in a big breath. What was she going to do with him?

She closed her eyes. *Lord, help us.* She knew she couldn't handle life on her own. But she often forgot to ask for help.

"Lank."

"Yes, babe?"

"You must get a hold of Matt and Kelly. Their two boys each have a broken arm. One had a fever. Don't you think the parents would want to know about their kids? Please reach them however you can figure it out. I've got to go to the cookhouse and help Lola bake cookies. Okay? Will you try again to call?"

"Is this where I say, 'Yes, Dear'?" He winked but also scrunched his shoulders and ducked, just in case.

As Carli entered the cookhouse kitchen the sight before her was a lot to take in. Mixing bowls, baking sheets, and multiple ingredients covered the counters. Lola's smile was dotted with flour.

"Great! Reinforcements. Here, put on an apron." Lola greeted her with a wide smile.

"Okay." Carli wasn't sure about all this. She was not a cook. Or baker. Whatever it was called. But Lola's good-natured confidence always bolstered her willingness to try.

"Where's the recipe to follow?"

"Oh, it's all in here." Lola pointed to her forehead.

"Seriously? How can anyone take over for you?"

Melodic laughter rose from Carli's ranch cook and dear friend.

"First of all, I hope no one will be taking my job any time soon. Second, I'm half-kidding. I do have some recipes written down. Over in that drawer. And I have a notebook I've been trying to organize. But for now, I'll be your guide. Go ahead and crack six eggs in that big bowl and we'll get started."

"What kind of cookies are we making?"

"Oh, chica, everything imaginable. Think Christmas! Red and green frosting. Sprinkles. Sugar cookies. Angel cookies. Here, put this Santa hat on to get you in the mood. I'll hit the music."

"I don't know about the hat, Lola. I'm good."

"That's an order. I am the master chef and you are my sous chef. The hat will also keep hair out of our cookies. I don't want the food inspectors to shut us down. You don't want to wear a dorky hair net, do you?" She gave Carli a playful grin.

"Fine." Carli pulled the Santa hat on.

And Lola sang "Deck the Halls!" with gusto. "Fa la la la la, la la la la."

"Hey, where are the boys?"

"Lank's got them for a while. I'm a little miffed

at him. Plus, to bring the boys over here could end up as a royal disaster. Talk about flour all over the place."

"Now, just a minute. I know exactly where everything is. I'm very organized. I just cook with abandon. Let the flour fall where it may." She closed her eyes, big smile of course, and held her hands out, palms up. Then she abruptly snapped out of it. "Wait. What did you say? You're miffed at Lank? Why?"

"I have asked him to contact his sister in London to tell her and Matt about the boys. They've got to know about their kids. Right?"

"Sure. Why doesn't Lank call?"

"He said he's tried, but gets no answer, no voice-mail. I'm not even sure he's calling the right number. Maybe they'd want to get on the next plane if they knew both boys had broken arms."

"Why do you think Lank hasn't gotten through to them?"

"I don't know. Is it a man thing?"

"Now, Carli, let's be fair. We can't be gender-prejudiced."

Carli squinted her eyes at Lola and cocked her head. "I've heard you say things about your husband in frustration. Like 'Buck can't cook' or 'Buck's stubborn'. How is this any different?"

"Maybe Lank's busy. Maybe he's afraid of Kelly being upset, that somehow, he didn't watch his nephews well enough. Maybe it's manly pride. There could be all kinds of reasons. You just need to talk to him. Didn't God say we were to be their helpmates?"

Carli rinsed her hands and picked up a towel to dry. "You've got to pull out the God card, don't you?" She gave a big sigh. "Okay. You're right."

"I can't stay quiet when God gives me a little nudge. It's my job to remind us to try to be patient with our grand *niños*." Lola flicked a little bit of flour at Carli's cheek.

"Don't start or we'll have a food fight in your kitchen."

"Why don't you just call Kelly? Sometimes we have to do things ourselves to make sure they get done."

Carli's fun mood started to darken. "Why do I have to do everything? I think I have my hands full as they are. Don't you?"

Just then Lola's cell phone played a rendition of "Hallelujah".

She quickly dusted off her hands with a towel and punched the green button to accept and also the microphone to put it on speaker. "Hello?"

"Aunt Lola? It's Rena."

"Well, hi, Rena. I'm here with Carli, baking. You're on speaker."

"Oh, hi, Carli. Listen, I've got some bad news."

"What is it, dear? Are you okay?"

"Yes, I'm fine. But it's my mom."

"Oh, my goodness, is Isabelle all right? Do I need to come?"

"She broke her ankle. In three places. Yesterday. The doctors are waiting for the swelling to go down some. But she's having surgery day after tomorrow." Then Rena snuffled and cleared her throat. In a small voice, she asked, "Can you possibly come, Aunt Lola?"

"Of course, Rena. I'll square things away here and then be on my way."

Then a flood of tears sounded through the

phone. "Thank you, Aunt Lola. That would mean the world to her, and me."

"How did it happen?"

"Just a crazy fluke. She was going down the front steps of her house to pick up her newspaper on the sidewalk. The steps were wet from an early rain, and she slipped. She's lucky she didn't break a hip or arms. But I guess not so lucky that her ankle is broken in three places. I hope she'll be okay. She is bruised all over."

"We'll pray, Rena. Don't worry. Okay?"

"Okay, Aunt Lola. Thank you so much."

When the call ended, Lola started to plan. "I'll have to talk to Buck. I might have to go alone if he can't . . . "

The door burst open. It was Lank with the nephews in tow.

"I was on the computer with the boys when another email from Kelly popped up. I can read it to you from my phone," Lank said. "It upset Zane."

Hi Boys, and Lank and Carli,

Hope everyone is well. Wanted to tell you – we're in Paris now! We wanted to celebrate our anniversary in a special way. I can't believe it's been ten years already. We'll try to send a picture of us kissing under the Eiffel Tower. It was SO romantic!

They say December is the rainiest month and we've had some sprinkles. Oh well. Chilly, too. Forty-seven degrees in the daytime. But it's still beautiful and the city is busy with people shopping and having fun.

We went to the Louvre Museum and saw the famous Mona Lisa painting by Leonardo da Vin-

ci. Is she smiling? Find her on the computer. The painter, da Vinci, was also a genius inventor. He worked on inventions like the parachute, a leather diving suit and breathing mask, and a giant crossbow, 27 yards across, that fired stones or flaming bombs. His sketches helped people in the 1940s invent the helicopter. He lived in 15th Century Italy. Isn't that amazing? Junior, I know you like to read about things like this.

Dad and I had such a great time in Paris. There are outdoor cafés with tables on the sidewalk. We had French Onion soup that was even better than what we make in America. Then delicious chocolates! You know how much I love chocolate.

We're trying to learn some French words. "Oui" means yes. It's pronounced "wee". Just don't say, "Wee wee." Don't laugh, boys! Another one is "Merci". It means thank you. Don't pronounce it like "mercy". Say it like a girl horse: "mare-see." Got it?

Our cell phones have been a little crazy. We'll have to go to the phone store when we get back. I'm glad I can send you this email. But we'll be away from the computer for a few days.

Remember to be good boys for Aunt Carli and Uncle Lank.

WE LOVE YOU WITH ALL OUR HEARTS!
Mom

Zane's face was red, and he rubbed tears from his eyes. "I wanna talk to my Mom. When is she coming home?"

Good grief. What next, Lord?

Chapter Forty

Carli

A blue box of macaroni thudded when it landed in the shopping cart and broke Carli out of her trance. She leaned down to look at her nephew eye to eye.

"Do you know how to count to ten?" she asked.

"Uh-huh." Zane nodded his head.

"I want you to get ten boxes of that mac and cheese and put them in our cart. In fact, I want you to get whatever else you like and put that in the cart too."

"But you only let me get one box last time."

The kid had a memory like an elephant. "That was weeks ago, and Lola is gone so we won't be able to enjoy her cooking. I don't think your parents will mind. This is an emergency."

A big grin washed over his face as he turned and carefully picked up one box, deliberately placing it in the basket. "One," he said proudly. "Oh wait. There's one in there already. Two. Three. Four." All the way to ten, macaroni boxes rattling after each addition. Carli glanced at her phone as she waited. *Patience please, Lord. This might take a while.*

"I should count them again to make sure."

"Absolutely," agreed Carli. What else do kids eat that would be easy for her? Sandwiches. Burgers, Spaghetti. That's it, every kid likes noodles, obviously. Boxed mac and cheese for lunch and spaghetti for supper. And then she said a silent prayer that the parents would be home soon.

She filled her basket with noodles, cans of sauce, and spice packets. A co-worker back in Georgia used them and had shared the instructions for an easy sauce. She had plenty of hamburger meat. Choosing lunch meat and vegetables, she remembered soup.

"Do you like chicken noodle soup, Zane?" He didn't answer because he wasn't behind her. Spinning her basket around, she pushed it forward and looked both ways to the end of the aisle. "Zane!"

He appeared from three aisles down balancing a box on his good arm. It was almost as big as he was.

"Do you like soup?" she asked again.

"No. But I like these." He held up a family-sized box of cheesy fish crackers.

"Perfect. Let's go," she said.

"Can we have a hot chocolate?"

"Of course. We can't come into Dixon without stopping to see Belinda."

At the checkout stand she kept shaking her head no as he held various items over the basket including gummies, chewing gum, bottle rockets, and chocolate bars, being careful to put each one back in its place before trying the next.

"I think we have enough," said Carli. "You can have a cookie at Belinda's." That seemed to satisfy him. She had created a shopping monster.

Before she could grab her purse and open her door, Zane was already pushing the coffee shop door open and then disappeared inside. She followed.

"Afternoon, you guys," Belinda said from behind the counter. "This young man has already placed his order. What can I get his awesome aunt?"

Carli laughed. "I believe I need a double shot of whatever you've got."

"Pumpkin spice is the most popular flavor, but we have a delicious peppermint and cocoa latte."

"I want that," said Zane.

"Are you sure you like peppermint?" Carli shook her head behind his back and Belinda nodded to show she agreed.

"How about marshmallows with that?" asked Belinda.

"And a cookie. Aunt Carli said so," Zane added.

"Well then, a cookie it is."

The coffee grinder buzzed. Carli lifted Zane up so that he could watch Belinda make their orders.

"What are you two doing?"

"Grocery shopping. Lola had to leave to take care of her sister. I need ideas to keep this crew fed. Easy recipes. Tell me what you've got. Go."

"You can always fix a big pot of spaghetti."

"I knew it," said Carli. "Kids like noodles, don't they?" She felt somewhat proud of herself for thinking of the idea first.

"You can't go wrong with noodles," said Belinda. "Are we all set for the Open House?"

"As far as I know. Thank goodness Lola finished several batches of cookies before she left, and with what you're bringing that should be enough."

"What are you making to drink?"

"A pot of coffee and maybe some crockpot spiced cider. Any ideas?"

"Oh, I think you'll need more than one pot. Everyone I've talked to is going. They are so excited. You're doing a good thing, Carli. The Wild Cow Ranch is an important part of this community."

"I just hope I can do my grandmother proud. How many years did she host this event? Do you know?"

"Let's see, I remember going to see the lights in junior high. My grandparents were visiting and we took them."

"Thanks, Belinda. We'll see you soon."

Zane followed her to the car, carefully sipping from his lidded cup and holding an iced Santa face in the other hand. Carli helped him into his car seat.

On the way back to the ranch, she thought about the scrapbooks in the back study. She should have paid more attention to the pictures. What she wouldn't give for a few photos from the Open House, just to get an idea of where they hung everything. The only information she could get from everyone she asked was there were lots of lights and it was beautiful. Where were the decorations? The fences, the trees, the house. Did she have Christmas trees in every room? So many possibilities. She didn't know where to begin.

And when had the tradition begun? And why? So many unanswered questions that she wanted to know. Instead of repeating, the only option she had was to create her own traditions because the past was gone.

After the groceries were put away, Carli cooked the hamburger meat. She wasn't sure how to measure servings, but three packages seemed enough for two growing boys plus her and Lank. Buck would probably join them too. She had to dump it into a larger skillet. The first one was too small.

On the floor in the pantry was her grandmother's cooker. She rinsed it out and filled it with water to boil the noodles. On the cooked meat she dumped five cans of sauce and sprinkled the mixture with the seasoning packets.

Enough spaghetti to feed the whole county, it looked like. Which was fine so she'd have leftovers and not have to cook that often, just reheat. Perfect plan.

Of course, the boys were anxious to check emails again.

Chapter Forty-One

Dear Boys, and Lank and Carli,

One night we tried the London Food Tour and tasted Indian food for the first time! It's not like our American Indians. These Indians are from the country India which is right below China and Pakistan. They use lots of curry which is a creamy and spicy sauce. Chicken Tikka Masala is the most popular Indian dish in England. It's roasted chicken chunks in a spicy curry sauce.

I liked it okay, but couldn't eat all of it. That curry was a little hot! Dad finished it for me.

WE LOVE YOU TONS! (and miss you!)
Mom

~~~

Dear Boys, and Lank and Carli,

The other day I got to go to Harrod's Department Store with the wife of one of Dad's co-workers. She was very nice to take me. Harrod's is super famous. It's the largest department store in Europe with ONE MILLION square feet. It was built in

1849. I liked the fact that in the old days they delivered purchases to customers by horse and carriage. That's pretty cool, isn't it?

Have you been able to go on a ride with Lank and Carli on one of their horses? Or, is it too cold there?

WE LOVE YOU WITH ALL OUR HEARTS! (and miss you!)

Mom

~~~

Dear Junior, Zane, and Lank and Carli,

Your dad and I got to see Stonehenge the other day. It's the world's most famous prehistoric monument. They say it was built about 5,000 years ago! It's a stone circle, but we're talking BIG stones! Some are thirty feet high and weigh twenty-five tons! BIG!! It's a mystery how it was built because way back then people didn't have bulldozers or other equipment like we do nowadays. Scientists figured out that some of these big stones, or pillars, were transported from 150 miles away. How was that possible back then? And how did the people get the stones to stand upright? Scientists say they used ropes to pull the stones up. That must have been really difficult! Other things I learned was that it took the builders 1,500 years to construct. Can you imagine? That's generations and generations of families all working on the same project.

It was a pretty area out in the country. Quiet and peaceful. Kind of strange to find these big stones out in the middle of nowhere.

WE LOVE YOU TONS! (as BIG as those stones!)
WE MISS YOU TOO!
Mom

Chapter Forty-Two

Taylor

"You ready, darlin'? We don't want to be late." Taylor was in the kitchen calling towards the adjoining dining room.

"I just want to write Shayla a note. Hope she sees it. I guess I should text but I don't want to bother her. What did you tell Hud?"

He walked to where she was seated at the dining room table and said, "To come to the Wild Cow when he's done with work. He can help me string some lights on the fences for Buck. I know they've got their hands full. What are you gonna be doing?"

"Oh, helping Lola and Carli with whatever they need. Probably baking cookies for one thing. Her grandparents used to hand out tons of them to all the visitors."

"And what about Shayla?" Taylor didn't like drama and was burdened lately with worry for her. Would she ever come around and accept Carli? They didn't have to be bosom buddies, just considerate.

"I'm not sure. I just hope she comes," Karissa said.

"Okay, you ready, darlin'?"

"Yes. Just gotta grab my jacket."

When they arrived at the Wild Cow, Taylor parked in front of the cookhouse. He gave Karissa a kiss on the cheek and they parted ways. "Don't eat too many cookies." Taylor winked. She headed inside to find Lola and Carli, and Taylor spotted Buck wrapping a light strand around a fence.

Taylor pulled his gloves on as he got closer. "Hey, whatcha doin', old man?"

"Easy now." Buck smiled. "I can run circles around you, desk jockey."

The men shook hands and Buck patted Taylor on the back. Before Carli and Lank had married and before Taylor found out he was her birth father, he and Buck had lost touch over the years. But now their friendship was being renewed and taking on a kindred, mature rhythm.

As a teen, Taylor had worked at the Wild Cow Ranch and dated Carli's mother, Michelle. Buck and Lola weren't that much older and Taylor always wondered if they had suspected his relationship with Michelle since the young lovers tried to hide it. A few months back, Buck had confirmed he and Lola always had a feeling about the couple.

"So, did'ja come to work or make fun of your elders?" Buck coughed a laugh. It was chilly outside.

Taylor chuckled. "I came to help so's you don't hurt yourself with that hammer."

"Oh, you're funny all right. Just watch yerself, cuz Santa's right around the corner."

"I have been a *very* good boy, I'll have you know." Taylor flashed a toothy grin.

"Hey, if you can be serious for one little minute," Buck said, "did you say on the phone that that son of yours was coming out too?"

"Yep. He's supposed to stop by after he finishes with a colt at Cross Creek. It's his day off but he wanted to put in a little time on him."

Buck's face looked serious. "That's the sign of a dedicated worker, for sure. You raised him right."

"He's a good kid. I can't complain."

Running across the lawn like a tornado came the nephews, tumbling and punching all the way. Broken limbs had not slowed them down one bit. Lank followed at a saunter.

Zane ran up to "Uncle" Buck, out of breath, sweaty dirty mark around his neck. "He's hittin' me! Tell 'im to stop!"

"Whoa, you little ruffians. Don't be runnin' me over. We've got things to do. And soon I'm gonna be puttin' you boys to work."

Zane looked up with wide, round eyes. "What's a rushy-in?"

Buck grinned. "Ruffian. Means all ya do is fight and carry on."

"That's us. We're like M-D-A fighters!" With that, Zane punched his brother in the stomach, to which Junior yelled, "It's MMA, you dork," and yanked Zane to the ground and pinned his shoulders to the ground.

Lank's voice was stern. "Do *not* do that, Junior. We don't want any more broken arms. Stand up and act right. Both of you."

In unison the boys said, "Sorry, Uncle Lank."

"C'mon over here and let's help Uncle Buck." Lank's face was devoid of patience.

"He's not really our uncle, is he?" Zane asked.

Lank said, "For now, he is. Now hold this strand while I try to untangle it. Junior, you walk with it real slow till I tell you to stop. Zane, stay right here."

The little boy looked from man to man, his head in constant motion. "What can I do? I want a job too."

Taylor and Buck exchanged glances, their eyes sparkling.

"I think you might need a lead line on those fellers," Buck joked with Lank who only shook his head and rolled his eyes.

"Maybe it's Carli's turn now," he said as they all watched Carli and Karissa walk up carrying plastic containers, two insulated, stainless-steel bottles, and a storage tote.

Carli announced, "We've got coffee or hot chocolate. What do y'all want?"

"And cookies! Lots and lots of cookies." Karissa bubbled with excitement. "We just need someone to sample them. I wonder who we could find."

"Me, me, me!" Zane's arm immediately went straight up as if in school.

Junior waited politely and held out his palm.

Carli smiled at Taylor. "Your wife saved the day. Lola had a family emergency, and I am so happy you two came out today. Karissa is going to help me with the last of the baking."

"Glad we can be a part of it," said Taylor. "Thanks for having us."

Karissa smiled, then looking to Taylor asked, "Where's Hud? Shouldn't he have been here by now?"

Taylor checked his black-faced watch. "Yeah. He must've gotten caught up in something. I don't have any texts from him. I'll try to call in a few minutes."

After the cookie, coffee, hot chocolate break, the ladies collected the cups and packed up the containers.

"It's cold out here. Let's go back inside," Karissa said. Then she turned to the pickup truck that was coming up the drive. "Oh, good, looks like Hud's here."

It was Hud's truck, but a young guy Taylor didn't recognize got out of the driver's side. When the passenger door opened and his son emerged, Taylor squinted. It looked like Hud was carrying something. *Oh, my God!* It was his arm.

Taylor and Karissa rushed over to him.

"What happened to you?" Taylor touched his son's shoulder.

"Oh, my goodness, are you all right?" Karissa was near tears.

"I'm fine. I'm fine. Just a misunderstanding with that colt this morning. He went this way and I went that'a way."

The little boys came running towards him, holding up their casted arms. "Look! Just like us!" Zane yelled.

"Hey now. You guys need to slow down. Hud, these are Lank's nephews Junior and Zane."

Hud chuckled. "Yeah, I guess all the cool kids have a cast." He held his arm up so that the boys could see it and then he bent over to admire theirs.

"Don't encourage these rascals." Buck shook his head but smiled.

Hud introduced his friend to everyone. "This is Jeremy. He works at Cross Creek and he's been at the ER with me when they put a cast on my arm. My phone was dead so I couldn't call."

"We're just glad you're okay, Son." Taylor kept his hand on Hud's shoulder, then shook hands with Jeremy. "Thanks a lot for staying with him. We appreciate it."

Karissa hovered. "What did the doctors say? Do you need surgery or anything? Does it hurt?"

"Mom, it's okay. Clean break. I'll need the cast maybe six weeks."

Zane rushed up. "Let's sign each other's casts!"

"Okay, little buddy." Hud smiled at both boys. "First, let's see how we can help. Even if we only have one workable arm."

Taylor stepped closer. "You can probably sit this one out. We've got it covered. And what about the horse? Is he okay?"

"Oh, yeah, he's fine. Just young and full of himself. I got between him and the fence, and the next minute my arm hit the fence hard, and then we heard a loud pop."

His friend Jeremy echoed that. "Yeah. It was a big crack."

The women made grimacing faces and collected their supplies. Carli and Karissa started to head to the cookhouse.

The ladies nodded. Karissa kissed Hud on the cheek and said, "Are you going home soon to rest, I hope?"

"Pretty soon, Mom, but I feel fine. Jeremy could take me home so I'll have my truck. The doctor didn't want me to drive. But someone will have to get Jeremy home."

"We can give him a ride," said Taylor. "You ladies need any help?"

With the break over, Taylor followed the girls

back to the cookhouse, carrying the tote for them. Karissa turned to Carli, "I left our daughter a note, but I'm not sure if she'll be able to help us today or not."

As they piled everything on the counter, Carli said, "I just want you both to know how much it means to me that y'all are here."

"It's important to Taylor that we become a part of your life, Carli." Karissa placed a hand on her shoulder. "It is an adjustment for all of us, but I hope that you'll be patient with us. Shayla is having a difficult time sharing her father. She's always been the apple of his eye."

"I would never want to come between you and your daughter," Carli said, unspoken concern reflecting in her eyes.

"It's all right. She'll come around," Taylor assured her.

Chapter Forty-Three

Mandy

Rapping on the glass entrance woke Mandy from a lazy mid-morning nap. She swung her legs over the side of the cot and shuffled out of the storeroom towards the main entrance.

"Sorry, we're closed until after the holidays," she called out.

The pounding didn't stop but grew louder. She walked closer and peeped out the side window to see Phin peering back at her. With a heavy sigh, she unlocked the door and moved so that he could step inside. Her hair was a stringy mess and she wore a stained shirt and huge sweatpants. She hadn't showered in a few days.

"We're closed, Mr. Shelton."

"I came by Tuesday and your car was here, but the door was locked."

"We didn't have any livestock come in this week. Calvin closed us down until after the first of the year. Why are you here?"

"I wanted to see if you were okay," he said smoothly. She sensed that he had an uncanny awareness about her and whatever she said next would be closely scrutinized.

"I'm doing just fine. You should go, Mr. Shelton." She gently pushed on his shoulder and tried to shut the door in his face, but he covered her hand with his.

"Mandy, let me in."

She glared at those blue eyes which caused her heart to thud, and that in turn triggered a step back. He walked past her, bringing with him the smell of musk cologne, fresh hay, and a cold winter day.

"Are you living here?"

So much for making small talk. Fear choked her throat and she put her arms protectively around her belly. "It's only temporary."

"Let me help you."

"I don't need your help." She faced him directly and looked him square in the eyes. "Take that back. I don't want your help. You need to stop bothering me or I will call the sheriff."

Guilt caused her heart to sting when she saw the hurt in his eyes. He was a good man. All the more reason he should stay as far away from her as he could.

"You talk big and tough, don't you? But the truth is I'm not going to leave you alone. I care about you, Mandy." He threw his hands up and turned to pace a few steps and then came back. "I know that's crazy. But I can't get you out of my mind. You're all I think about, day and night. I can't eat. I can't sleep."

"Why do I attract the psychos? Look at you. All handsome and nice, flashing those blue eyes my way and then you go crazy. Typical. I'm calling the sheriff." She spun on her heel and marched into the office. It was certainly hard to act tough like you mean business when you have to waddle away. Thank goodness they had a landline because her cell phone had been cut off last week. She felt a little safer with the desk between them.

"I'm not a psycho, Mandy. You know it. I'm here because I think you feel something too. Look me in the eye and tell me you don't." He focused on her face with a critical squint.

The truth was she was exhausted from trying to sleep in that cold storeroom on that hard cot. She was hungry. She needed a shower. And she'd never be able to buy enough diapers to last more than a couple of months. Everything this baby needed was so expensive. Despite her tough exterior, she was about to have a nervous breakdown. Her whole body was weighed down in weariness and despair.

She looked into his eyes and saw honesty, decency, and a man who worked hard for what he wanted. She also saw something there she'd never seen in a man's eyes before. Love. Respect. At that point she burst into tears and sank back into the office chair. Heavy sobs took over her body. She was powerless to stop. Who was acting like the psycho now?

Phin scooted a chair close and sat down. Facing her, he wrapped his arms around her shoulders. She leaned close and wrapped her arms around him, burying her face in his neck. He didn't speak for several long moments, letting her cry until there was nothing left.

"You do feel something for me, don't you?" he muttered into her ear.

"It's pregnancy hormones. It's not real. A person doesn't fall in love in just a few weeks." But that wasn't true. She had fallen hard for Jeff the moment she laid eyes on him, and she had to admit there had been an attraction for Phin too. But she wasn't the same woman she had been before. Love wasn't some fairytale and she'd never pine over a man ever again. She would not let herself be that weak.

"You know I prayed for you."

"So has my mother's Sunday school class. You see how that worked out." She snorted.

"No, I mean I prayed for someone just like you. Someone who could handle the work of being a rancher's wife. Someone who is beautiful inside and out, and who could be happy in a life with me without kids."

She wiped her face with one sleeve and blinked away tears. "What do you mean without kids?"

"I had an injury as a young boy and odds are I will never be able to have children of my own. So, I prayed that He might bless me with someone who really needed me and who I could make a huge difference in their life. God sent me you."

Mandy sat back in the chair and stared at him. She needed a minute to digest what he just said. Her first inclination was to remind him she wasn't some charity case, but the emotions on his face told it all. His confession broke all rules of logic and reason. Yet her heart swelled with a feeling she had never imagined she would feel again for any man.

"I know your heart, Mandy. We haven't known each other that long, yet I know everything about you."

She nodded. "I know you too."

"Get your things. You're coming home with me."

"No."

"Why not? I will not allow you to stay here. This is no place for a lady and the mother of my child."

Those were fighting words. "First of all, you're not my daddy and I don't have to ask you permission to do anything. Secondly, if your parents are as religious as you sound, then they'll never accept me if you bring me home now. Broke, unmarried, and pregnant. They will always see me as the girl out for your money. Let's take this slow. I need to feel more confident about myself and our relationship before you push me on to your parents."

His face fell.

"I lived with my mother for eighteen years. I know how strict parents can be about the things they want for their children," she said.

"Will you agree to let me take you to the women's shelter? You'll have a bed and a shower, three meals a day. I will give you a ride to your next doctor's appointment."

"How do you know about such a place? I've never heard of it."

"Our family has donated to the shelter for years. My father once served on the Board."

"I don't need your charity."

"I'll call right now and reserve a bed for you. Let's get your things."

Panic suddenly hit Mandy as she stood and walked to the storeroom. Phin followed with an arm around her shoulder, but she was so ashamed that he would see where she had been sleeping. He didn't bat an eye though.

She stopped. "I'm not leaving." She made the rules for her life now, not a man. She'd never play victim again.

"I promise to love this boy as my own, Mandy."

"I know you will, Phin. This doesn't mean I'm not interested in you. This means that I have to stand on my own feet, my own terms. We hardly know each other and you're already ordering me around."

"We can take it slow, if you want. I can back off a bit."

"I would appreciate that." She walked closer until the smell of him erased the moldy odors of the back storeroom. Rising on her tiptoes, she gently kissed his mouth. Reclaiming her lips, he crushed her to him, baby in between. The fire between them rose to a new level.

He stepped back, his eyes wide with shock.

"Wow," she said.

"No kidding, wow. What was that?"

She giggled.

Without hesitation, he moved in for more. His kisses sang through her veins. She'd never been kissed like that before.

Pausing to catch her breath, she said, "I'm not moving out of the sale barn just because you say."

"Okay," he said. "Whatever you want." He leaned in but she put her hands on his chest.

"I'll decide when and where I should live. I'll do the best thing for me and my son."

He nodded that he understood. "There's something I need you to do for me."

She looked deep into his eyes and her heart dropped to her knees. This handsome cowboy promised a future of love and a life for her and her child. She couldn't believe how he had dropped into her life from nowhere, like a bright, shining beam of light during the most wretched days. She never saw it coming. And she knew she would love him until the day she died.

"All right. What can I do for you?"

"I need you to introduce me to your mother."

Chapter Forty-Four

Carli

"Boys. That's enough racket." She scooted them away from her computer. "I have some work to do today and then you can help me decorate the tree."

They had taken the boys to early church services on Wednesday night with Buck since Lola was still gone, and then they had taken them to their favorite place for dinner. Whataburger in Amarillo, of course. While there, they had stopped at Kelly and Matt's house to check on things, get more dog food, and they allowed the boys to pick up some of their electronics. She had to admit they did have a good selection of movies, and the boys picked out a handful of their favorites.

Lank buzzed through the kitchen on his way out, filling his thermos and then stopping in the office to give Carli a kiss on the cheek.

"Need anything from me today?" he asked.

"If you have a chance, would you mind buying several more extension cords? I think we'll need a few more before Saturday."

"Sure. No problem. I need to check salt blocks

this morning, and then I'll head into town around noon. I think Buck is hauling hay for the horses. He's around, if you need anything."

"Spaghetti for lunch," she said.

"Don't worry about me. I'll grab something somewhere." He avoided her eyes.

She laughed. Lank wasn't as big a fan of spaghetti as his nephews. They might all turn into a noodle before Lola got back.

Finally, with the boys watching a movie, she propped her feet into a dining room chair and took a slow sip of coffee. She closed her eyes and took a deep breath to relax a few more minutes before she started dragging out decorations for the Christmas tree. It looked lonely and bare sitting in one corner of their living room. Her phone buzzed. Of course, it was back in her bedroom still plugged into the outlet. She answered, a bit out of breath from hurrying.

"We're looking for Lank Torres," the voice said.

"This is Mrs. Torres. Can I help you?"

"This is the Monkey Wrench Garage, and we delivered your car back to the sale barn last week. That'll be $650.85. Mr. Torres asked us to bill him, but we forgot to get a mailing address."

Carli's blood ran cold. Lank was paying for Mandy's car repair? She cleared her throat and gave them the address.

"Thanks, ma'am. We appreciate your business."

Her first thought was to call Lank right away, but she had dogs and boys listening in. This was way more important than a phone call or text. She needed to look him in the eye and confront him. But then she started thinking. The root of the problem wasn't Lank per se.

Maybe it was time she confronted the issue and went straight to the horse's mouth so to speak. Maybe it was time she had a little chat, girl to girl.

She punched in Buck's number. "It's Carli. Can you watch the boys for a few minutes? I need to run an errand."

Carli pulled into a parking spot in front of the sale barn and walked slowly towards the entrance, taking note of Mandy's car. She veered towards it, peering inside as she passed. It was as if she were looking into someone's life. The car bulged with junk. Well, maybe junk to Carli, but obviously everything the girl owned. The back piled with mostly clothes, the front seat stacked with tennis shoes, sandals, and several pairs of boots. On one side of the backseat, a collection of baby stuff including a few jumbo packs of diapers. Those would come in handy.

For a minute she felt her heart soften with sympathy, and then she remembered why she was here. Mandy needed to find another support system other than Lank. Carli knew he would never tell her no, so she had decided to take things into her own hands. Confronting the girl at her workplace was not the best of situations, but maybe they could go somewhere and talk. Perhaps she could follow Mandy home, or maybe she would agree to something to drink at the drive-in.

It looked like everyone had gone already, but Carli tried the front entrance anyway. It was unlocked so she went in. She looked through the glass at the counter in the business office, but she didn't see Mandy anywhere. The cement floor was covered in dust which coated the bottom of Carli's jeans as she walked towards the sale arena. The smell of manure and Texas dirt made her nose tickle. A quick scan of the stadium seats and the front auctioneer's box did not turn up results either. The showroom was empty. She had left her house in such a hurry after she got her courage up to confront the girl, she now needed to use the restroom after the long drive.

In a back hallway through a door marked LADIES, one bulb hung from a cord. As she washed her hands, she heard a noise. A girl talking, but when she shut the water off it stopped. She reached for a paper towel and heard the noise again, but it wasn't talking. It sounded more like sobbing. Carli stood still and listened, focusing on the sound and from where it might be coming. Definitely someone crying.

Careful not to let the bathroom door slam, she stepped into the dank hallway. The next door read CLOSET. She gently pushed it open.

Mandy sat on a low cot that was covered with a threadbare blanket, wiping her face with her shirtsleeve. Her head and shoulders slumped forward, she stared at the ground, and didn't even hear Carli push open the door.

"Are you all right?" Carli asked.

The very pregnant girl looked up with a start, eyes wide with fright. She swallowed and wiped her snotty nose with the other sleeve. She didn't speak.

"I've been looking for you," Carli said. "We need to talk."

"I know who you are, and I know why you're here," Mandy said. "We have nothing to talk about.

Leave me alone."

"Lank's my husband."

"I know." Mandy's eyes glinted sharp and mean. She stood. "I have things to do, and we're closed."

"Are you okay?"

"How I'm doing is none of your business." Mandy shoved past her and into the hall.

"Actually, it is." Carli spun around and stepped directly into her path. "You've been calling my husband a lot. That is my business. I know you have a history and that you used to date, but he's married now."

Mandy's jaw clenched and she raised her chin to glare back at Carli. "I can't deal with you right now." She walked around Carli and disappeared through a door at the end of the hall marked EMPLOYEES ONLY. Carli followed.

"Wait. We need to talk about this."

They were standing outside in the covered corral behind the sale barn.

"Fine. Say it." Mandy spit the words out.

"You have to stop calling my husband." Carli's heart thudded hard in her chest, but she'd said the words she came to say. Despite the look of utter sadness on Mandy's face, Carli stood her ground, confident in her words. Girlfriends cannot keep contacting their ex-boyfriends.

Mandy's chest heaved and fresh tears covered her cheeks.

Carli suddenly felt like the most horrid person in the world. She stepped closer and wrapped her arms around Mandy. "Is it time for you to go home? I can take you. Let's go back inside where it's warm."

The silence seemed awkward and deadening in

the small hallway.

"Mandy. Talk to me," said Carli.

"Calvin lets me sleep on the cot in the supply room, but this baby is due in several weeks. Where am I going to keep an infant then? I can't raise my son in a sale barn. I think that I have a new boyfriend, but he wants to boss me around too and look at me. I'm not sure why he would want someone like me."

"I had no idea of your situation. Lank never told me."

"Lank doesn't know. No one knows. I told my boss that my apartment is being remodeled."

"Oh, Mandy."

"I only called your husband because I was desperate. Lank is a good guy and I knew he would get my car running or take me to the doctor's appointment."

"That's one thing we can agree on. He is a good guy."

"I want to raise my son on my own terms and make my own decisions, but now I'm thinking it might be impossible."

"You may not believe this, but I understand about being alone. That's why you're going home with me."

"No! I can't."

"You can talk big, but you're not winning this one," said Carli. "I've been on my own much longer than you and I am used to getting my way."

"I am exhausted," muttered Mandy.

Carli could see her wilting. Dark circles were under eyes red from crying, and her shoulders slumped. It looked like she might fall over any minute. Carli knew it wouldn't take much more convincing to get her in the pickup truck.

"Let's grab what you need from your car. I'm taking you back to the Wild Cow Ranch."

Even through the tears, Carli saw a ray of hope light her eyes. She nodded her head.

"Can I borrow your phone?" she asked. "I need to call my boyfriend."

"Of course, you can use it to call anyone you'd like. And, Mandy, you are not alone." Carli marched past her and outside to the truck. She needed to text Lank and tell him what she'd done.

Chapter Forty-Five

Carli

Carli and Mandy stood in the middle of the living room in Lank's old trailer house. Located at the back of ranch headquarters behind the saddle house, Carli's grandfather had bought the trailer for him when he became the full-time ranch hand.

"I think you'll be comfortable here and you'll have some privacy. Here's an old land line phone. I will jot my cell phone number down for you. Here's the thermostat. You can set it to whatever you want. It feels cold to me, but I hear that pregnant women are always hot."

Mandy stood in the center of the room slowly spinning around and holding a trash bag of clothes, unshed tears glistening in her eyes.

"It still looks like a bachelor pad. I haven't had time to redecorate, but the bed is already made up with clean sheets. I think there is soap and shampoo in the bathroom, but it may be only men's products. Sorry about that." She made a pass through the bathroom to double check.

Still no response from the young girl so Carli

kept rattling on. "You're welcome to join us for lunch or dinner, or both. It's spaghetti."

A half-smile and a curious glance crossed Mandy's face, so Carli explained, "I'm not the world's best cook, but I have discovered that Lank's nephews will eat noodles so I made a huge pot of sauce. All I have to do is cook the pasta. It's a time-saver."

"I shouldn't have come here," Mandy said, her voice flat and sad. She remained in the middle of the room, tense and stiff with a deep frown on her face.

"I'm sorry if you feel that I bullied you." Carli perched on the end of a stool.

"Well, you caught me at a weak moment. I had just told someone else that I could make my own decisions."

"You look exhausted. I wanted to get you somewhere you could rest, and this bed is empty, so this is the first place I thought of."

"I don't know why I let you talk me into coming with you. I'm not sure if this is a good idea."

"Okay, let's start over." Carli walked closer to Mandy.

"We have this empty trailer house that no one is using, and it's here if you need it. Lank and I would be thrilled if you stayed here, and you can stay for as long as you like. You decide."

Mandy's expression froze, her face pale, and then she glanced around the room again.

"If this isn't going to work, just tell me. I will take you back to the sale barn." Carli turned her back to allow Mandy some space to compose herself. She opened the fridge, but she knew it had been cleaned out some time ago. In the small pantry, there were some energy bars but that was it.

"I just realized, if you dated Lank you might have been here before." She set the bars on the kitchen cabinet and shut the pantry door. Leaning one hip against the cabinet, she crossed her arms.

"No, I've never been here," said Mandy. "Honestly, Lank and I didn't date that long. I pursued him, but he wasn't that interested."

Carli was relieved at that news, not that it mattered anymore.

"I'm sorry that I kept texting and calling your husband, but he really got me out of a jam. He took me to my doctor's appointment."

"That's what he told me. I didn't realize that you were alone during this pregnancy and I'm sorry for confronting you the way I did." Carli sincerely meant that, and she regretted the little temper fit she had thrown earlier.

Mandy shrugged and smiled. "You were just taking up for your man. At the time I was furious, but now I think it's very sweet. How did you know Lank was the one?"

"I knew it probably the first moment we met, but I spent almost a year arguing with myself about it. I was the heir and new ranch owner. He was the cow puncher. If I was going to be taken seriously as the new boss, dating an employee would undermine everything I wanted to achieve. In the end, he won me over."

"So, he pursued you?"

"Yes. He says he knew that I was the one from the very first moment we met and wasn't interested in anyone else. If I had just followed my heart after that first kiss." Carli laughed.

"Do you believe in love at first sight?" Mandy

finally gave in and sat down in the easy chair.

"I have asked myself that question over and over. There was no doubt about a spark between Lank and I, but I think your head has to take over too. Common sense says that you don't even know this person. They're a complete stranger, and yet you're willing to give up everything and take a chance. I prayed about Lank many times. I had this overwhelming peace about him, and when we were together it felt right. I knew this was where God wanted me to be."

Mandy stared at the wall in front of her for several minutes. She stood and wandered down the hall, stopping to look inside the bathroom and then walking into the bedroom. She turned and headed back towards Carli.

"It seems fine. Thank you. The selling point is that bed," she said with a chuckle.

"That's good. I'm glad. Is there anything else you need?"

"I think I'd like to sleep. That cot hasn't been the most comfortable." Mandy walked towards the bedroom and placed a trash bag on the bed. "This looks really nice. Thank you."

"You are so welcome. I'll be back to check on you later and bring you some groceries. We are keeping Lank's nephews while his sister is in Europe, and I hate to pass them off to Buck for too long. Buck is my ranch foreman."

"I'll be fine. Thank you."

Carli glanced around the room one more time but couldn't think of anything else to say or do so she gave Mandy a quick hug and left. The girl was most definitely overwhelmed and shell-shocked.

Lank pulled into the driveway at the same time

that Carli did.

"Did you get Mandy settled?"

"Yes, I did. I had no idea that she didn't have any family to help her. And did you know the sale barn is closed until after the first of the year? She's been sleeping in the back storeroom on a cot. Who is her mother? Where is her family?"

"I remember her dad. He was really nice, but passed. Her mom is sweet," said Lank as he held the front door open for Carli. "Mandy and her mother had a falling out. I'm not even sure what it was about."

"I'm sorry I doubted you, Lank. Of course, we should help any of your friends, including ex-girl-friends. I have no doubt that's quite a long list." She laughed at the look of innocence that he tried to fake.

"Let's bring up your list of old boyfriends then," he teased.

"That's easy. There aren't any. I was chasing show ribbons. Didn't have time for boys. Except one, but I've completely gotten over him. Can't even remember his name." She wrapped her arms around her husband's waist and lay her cheek on his chest.

"You think you're so smooth. Please tell me, lovely wife, that we are not having spaghetti again for lunch."

Carli turned loose and walked into the kitchen. She opened the refrigerator and studied the contents. Buck would be joining them too. Cooking was just not one of her favorite things.

"I'm hungry," said Zane as he slid to a stop in his sock feet.

"Me too." Junior followed close behind.

Carli shut the fridge door and turned to face them. "Your Uncle Lank is going into town to pick us up a pizza. Aren't you, dear?"

"Carli. That's a thirty-minute drive into Dixon and then back."

"Be sure and get enough. We have six people to feed." She grinned and wiggled her eyebrows.

His shoulders fell as he looked at her with pleading eyes. She stared back.

"Fine. Will you call it in?"

"Yes, I will. Okay, guys. What do you like?"

"Pepperoni!"

"Sausage!"

"Can we have extra cheese?"

Carli punched in the number and placed their order and then she texted Buck to let him know the pizza would be at her house.

Lank put back on his boots and grabbed his coat and hat from the entry hall. Carli opened the front door and gave him a kiss on his cheek. "Thanks. I'm kinda tired of my spaghetti too." She laughed.

As he drove away, Carli looked across the compound and noticed a nice pickup truck parked in front of the trailer house. Maybe that was Mandy's boyfriend.

Darn, that means seven people for lunch and then she chided herself for being a bit selfish. Whatever you need me to do, Lord.

To the boys she said, "Let's check our emails while we wait for Uncle Lank. Maybe your mother had time to send something. And then you can help me take some groceries over to Mandy."

She followed Junior and Zane into her office.

Chapter Forty-Six

Dear Boys and Lank and Carli,

Sorry we haven't sent any emails for a few days. We went to Paris and didn't want to take our computer since we were going to be sightseeing. So, we had it locked in the safe at the London hotel.

We had a wonderful time and I'll show you all the pictures when we get home. That is, IF we can get our pictures back.

I have a little bit of bad news. While we were in Paris, pickpockets stole my phone. And I had been taking all of our photos—in London and in Paris— with the phone.

Pickpockets are thieves who steal your wallets or phones or whatever they can get their hands on. Most of them are so good at their crime that you don't even feel when they are putting their fingers in your pockets or purse. Lots of people had warned us to be cautious. They said a lot of the pickpockets are gypsies and they don't work. Instead, they steal from others. It's very bad. We were not hurt and did not even know when they stole from us. They got both my phone and your Dad's.

The good thing . . . I hope it works . . . is that your Dad said our photos are saved to the Cloud. He knows how all of that works so once we can go to the phone store and get new phones, we'll see if they can retrieve our photos. I would be sad if they are lost. But we're hoping for the best.

We also have another bit of bad news. We may not make it home in time for the Christmas Open House at the ranch. I'm really sorry about this. We're trying to figure it out. Your Dad has been working on a really important project and he is so good at what he does. But the project is taking more time to complete and they've run into a few problems. He's got to stay until it's all figured out.

We've talked about whether maybe just I should come home to make it there by Christmas. But I hate to leave your Dad.

Boys, please know that we LOVE you with all our hearts and we MISS YOU tons. We want to come home and be with you, especially with Christmas coming soon. But we also have to figure out these adult problems with your Dad's job.

Please remember to say a prayer that God will work it all out.

Love,

Mom and Dad

Chapter Forty-Seven

Mandy

Her name floated on the breeze of a warm spring day. The voice low and gentle. She imagined a meadow of wildflowers and sunshine on her face.

"Mandy." A shake to her shoulder which she shrugged away. "Wake up, sweetheart."

No. She didn't want to leave the warm, sunny place.

"It's me. Phin. Wake up."

"Phin?" Mandy blinked in an effort to remember where she was. She didn't recognize the room and closed her eyes again. The bed was so soft and warm. She wanted to sleep for a few minutes more.

"Mandy. I need to ask you something." Phin patted her shoulder and then kissed her forehead.

She rolled over in disgust. Why couldn't everyone just leave her alone? Where was she? Oh, yes. The Wild Cow Ranch in Lank's trailer. Lank is married to Carli. She's so nice. And then little man reminded her of his presence after she had changed positions. Mandy shot out of the bed, barely making it to the bathroom in time.

"What are you doing here?" she asked, as she made her way back to that warm cocoon that she regretted having to abandon.

"I have something to ask you."

"Make it quick. I'm exhausted and I'm going back to sleep," She said, pulling the covers under her chin and closing her eyes.

"Mandy. Look at me," he said.

She blinked. And there he was, sitting on the floor right next to the bed with a big grin and a glimmer in his eyes, like he knew a secret and she didn't.

"What is it, Phin?"

"Will you marry me?"

Her eyes popped open in an instant, she focused, and there he was, kneeling on one knee next to the bed holding a sparkling diamond ring between his thumb and forefinger.

She sat straight up in bed and blinked again, her mouth open.

"I love you, Mandy. Let's get married. What do you say?"

"I don't know what to say."

"First of all, I'm glad that you're not still staying at the sale barn in the storeroom. I'm thankful that you called me and let me know where you were going. Secondly, I'm not pressuring you into anything you don't want. Just listen to your head and your heart."

She studied his face, so confident and full of love for her. Where did this man come from? The harder she tried to ignore the truth the more it persisted. This unexplainable ease that she felt around him, like she had known him all her life, broke the barriers that guarded her heart.

"I've been praying about us," Phin said. "I want

to give you and your unborn child a home. I know this is right."

She wanted to say yes. With every fiber of her whole being, she wanted to say yes and get on with her life. But the hurt of the past still had its daggers in her mind and soul. All men were liars. That is what she knew for a fact.

"I was wrong to order you around. I am sorry. We are partners in life. I should have asked you about what you want. And now I'm asking you this. Will you say yes, and will you consider getting married to me this afternoon?"

She stared at him with wide eyes, her heart thudding in her chest. That was the most ridiculous thing she had ever heard. And then he leaned forward and pressed his lips against hers. She kissed him back with a hunger that belied her outward calm and all the excuses for saying no vanished in an instant. He pulled back in surprise.

"That is not a kiss from a woman who is going to say no." His eyes, a startling blue, crinkled at the sides as his face broke into a broad grin.

She laughed. "You said this afternoon?"

"Yes. My father is a deacon at the Christian Church, but he also fills in for weddings and funerals. I told my parents all about you last night. They are really excited to meet you. The church is available later this afternoon. I'm not sure about your mother though. Do you want her there too?"

"No. My mother and I are still too complicated. Maybe we can go by her house another day."

"There's one thing you should know about me." Phin got off the floor and sat on the bed next to her. "When I make my mind up about something, I'm like a bulldog. I am relentless. If you say no and you feel rushed, that's okay, but I will be a part of your life from this day forward and I will wait until you're ready. I will take whatever you have to give me."

The sincerity on his face brought tears to her eyes. "Yes," she whispered. "Today."

He carefully put the ring on her finger. "This was my grandmother's."

The next few moments were a whirlwind of activity as Phin jumped up and hollered. "All right! Let's get going. I'll call my dad and tell him it's a go." He turned and faced her. "You have made me the happiest man ever. It's you, me, and a precious little boy. I am so proud of my family. You jump in the shower. I will make some phone calls."

She stared at him and crossed her arms.

"I'm sorry. I'm ordering you around again. What time will you be ready to leave, dear?"

She laughed. "Give me thirty minutes." An ache moved over her as she realized she didn't have anything to wear, but she wasn't going to let that ruin her happiness. They would be just as married in boots and jeans versus a tuxedo and formal gown.

Within the hour, Mandy and Phin were on their way to the church where they would exchange vows. Mandy's stomach was a flurry of butterflies and baby. Even little man seemed to be more active than usual.

"I can't make any sense of this thing between us, either," Phin said. "I have prayed and prayed, and God has put this on my heart to not wait any longer. I have no doubts."

They pulled into the parking lot of a simple

church building, light brick with one end that rose to a point and held a cross at the top. Mandy was suddenly terrified. Phin parked and hurried around to open her door. He helped her to the pavement and clasped her hand in his.

"Oh, let me have the ring back," he said with a chuckle.

Inside, they were greeted by a nice-looking couple. "These are my parents. Mom. Dad. This is Mandy."

He had gray hair, very distinguished looking, and she had blonde hair fashioned in a bun on top of her head. Phin got his blue eyes from his mother. The smiles on their faces and the happiness in their eyes were sincere. Mandy got the impression that they were genuinely happy for their son.

"If you'll come with me, I've got a dress for you," his mother said. "And you can call me Doris."

"Oh, forgive my manners. My dad's name is Bert," Phin said.

She followed Doris to a back hallway and into the ladies' room. Hanging on one of the stall doors was the most beautiful dress she had ever seen in a soft peach. "Is this for me?"

"My sister, who you'll meet, owns a secondhand shop. It's not new, but it's long and flowing, and big enough for . . . er."

"To cover my belly." Mandy laughed. "It's beautiful. Thank you."

With Doris's help she slipped the dress over her head. A bag emerged with makeup, which Doris helped her apply. "You don't need much. You're a beautiful girl." Mandy felt her cheeks warm.

She stood still while Doris applied a bit of hairspray to fluff up her long hair around her face.

"I think this shade of lipstick," she said.

Mandy looked at the woman for a minute and then said, "I do love your son, you know. We haven't known each other that long, but I feel in my heart that this is the right thing to do. I know it must be a shock."

Doris stopped spraying for a minute and looked back at Mandy's reflection in the mirror. "We are thrilled to see Phin so happy. He's undergone a complete transformation. If that's because of you, then we welcome you into our family. Our son does not make irrational decisions. He never has. He is steadfast and true."

"Yes, I've realized that about him."

"Are you ready?" Doris asked.

Mandy nodded her head and followed the woman to the sanctuary. Doris walked to the front of the church and sat behind the piano. At the altar stood Bert and Phin. Mandy paused at the door for a minute, not sure what she should do next. Another woman stood on the opposite side of Phin. Doris began to play the bridal procession. Bert motioned at Mandy to step forward.

Slowly and deliberately, she walked down the center aisle, distracted for a moment by the elaborate lead glass windows that lined both sides. Simple gold chandeliers hung overhead.

It surprised her that she didn't want to bolt and run, but she sensed a calm and peace that she had never felt before. She focused on Phin's face, and he never once took his off her. As she grew closer, she saw traces of tears on his cheeks.

The exchange of vows was simple and direct,

typical for the man she was marrying.

Mandy said, "I do."

Phin said, "I do."

And they were pronounced married. Phin's parents hugged her and welcomed her to the family. Phin offered to buy everyone's dinner.

"I'm calling my sister and invite them too," said Doris.

The woman who stood as witness was the church secretary, and she seemed delighted at the dinner invitation.

And so began the next chapter of Mandy's life. Little man had a daddy.

Chapter Forty-Eight

Carli

"Aunt Carli." Her name hissed on the air and invaded her dreams.

She heard her name but did not want to open her eyes. A smack on her cheek did it and then a small light hit her right in both eyes. She squinted.

"Aunt Carli." Zane stood by her side of the bed waving his small flashlight. Behind him the room was still black as pitch outside.

"What is wrong?"

"I'm cold." He lifted the covers and crawled in as she scooted closer to her husband's warm back.

Everything about her nephew was frigid. The one arm without cast, legs, and his feet were like ice cubes. "Did you knock the covers off?"

"My bedroom is too cold."

"Okay, you're all right now. Lie still and go back to sleep."

Within minutes, his soft snores almost lulled her back to sleep too. Almost. A giant ball of hair landed at the foot of her bed along with Lily Jane who crawled up in between Carli and Lank to lie on his pillow.

"Good grief." She stared into the blackness of the early morning, and then wondered what had happened to the nightlight in the hallway. She usually kept it on for the boys.

Sitting straight up in bed the cold made her nose tingle. She reached over and patted her husband's shoulder. "Lank. The power's out."

And then realization hit.

Her shoulder slumped and she lowered her head. Please, no.

The electricity cannot be out on the day of the Open House. All those thousands of bulbs and all the extension cords they had hunted for were all useless now.

"Lank. You have to call Lester."

The elusive Lester who works for the utility company and is assigned to their section of the grid. Thunderstorms, lightning, rain, high winds, and ice storms can all contribute to a line breaking. The problem with where they lived, there were miles and miles of line before it reached ranch headquarters. Finding where the problem happened was sometimes more challenging than repairing it.

"Lank. We have to help Lester find where the break is on the line."

Lank moaned. "One more minute."

She crawled over a sleeping Zane to find her sweatshirt that she had left on the floor.

"Aunt Carli."

"Go ahead and get in on my side, Junior. Are you cold, too?"

Another light hit her square in the face which made her look down, but with enough light to find her shirt and sweatpants. She pulled them on over her pajamas.

"It's freezing in here," he said.

She lifted the covers and he crawled in over his brother. She tucked them both in. She needed big fuzzy socks and her slippers, and probably another shirt. Brrrr.

In the kitchen she turned on every gas burner on the stovetop. That would have the kitchen warm in no time. Grabbing her phone for light, she went to the back study and built a fire in the pot belly stove that stood in one corner. Searching through the top desk drawer for a sticky note that had Lester's phone number, she had to hold up several slips of paper and shine her phone light to find the right one. She would make sure Lank saw it when he woke.

By the time the first rays of light cast glimmers through the windows, she had the campfire coffee on the stovetop ready. It tasted a tad bitter, but strong and good. The only thing she could think of to cook was bacon and scrambled eggs. With a blanket wrapped around her waist, Carli sat at the table and propped her feet on another chair. Releasing a big sigh, she said a silent prayer. "Please Lord, help Lester find the problem so that we can have power for the Open House."

So much for the miles of power cords that ran across the headquarters. The lights strung on every fence and on every building were useless now. Just in case the power could not be restored, she needed all hands on deck and a plan B to boot. The cookies were done. She could set up tables and lanterns on the front porch. Extra tables and chairs were already stacked in the garage.

And then she remembered the countless antique luminaries in the basement. Of course! Everyone just might have to settle for an old-fashioned Christmas. The problem now was could she find enough candles. She needed a big, bright spotlight like she'd seen at concerts. They run on their own generator and light up an entire football field.

What was the next best thing? She sipped her coffee and thought.

Bonfire! They needed a massive bonfire burning in the front yard for light and heat. It would be perfect. Call this an old-fashioned family Open House and a step back in time. She jumped to her feet.

"Lank! I need you to build a fire in the front yard. Get up, boys. We have to carry up some stuff from the basement and I need your help. Let's get going!"

"More junk from the basement?" complained Junior from under the covers.

She lit an old lantern that sat on her grandmother's dresser. The light illuminated three heads buried deep under the covers, and two dogs watched her with uninterested, drooping eyes.

"Come on, guys. Let's get cracking!"

She needed to call Buck. And she might try her father too. Maybe Taylor and Karissa could come early and help. The odds of them having electricity before mid-afternoon were slim, so she had to think about an alternative. This could be saved. This could still be the best Open House the Wild Cow Ranch had ever hosted.

That was her silent prayer anyway.

Several hours later, the To Do list swarming in her head, Carli decided to walk over to the cookhouse and lay out all the cookies on serving trays.

Lola had stored them in the walk-in freezer before she left. They should be thawed and ready to eat by late afternoon.

She paused on the front porch to watch Buck struggling with a flat-bed trailer load of figurines. He had pulled to a stop directly in front of her house and was unloading items in her front yard.

"What is that?"

"A life-sized Nativity! Isn't it grand?"

"Where in the world did you get that?"

"From the local junior college. It's from their theatre department and it's been in storage. Might need a little repair work on the wooden manger, but I think we can make it work."

Carli stepped up into the back of the trailer to help him with one of the Wise Men. "They're heavy."

"Stone-resin, they tell me. They look real, don't they?"

Carli laughed at his enthusiasm. "You did good, Buck."

"The camel is actually painted on a board, but I think he's my favorite."

It wasn't a crude painting like Carli first imagined, but instead, a work of art. The detail on his eyes, nose, and fur was unbelievable. He had a bright orange blanket over his hump, with a detailed fringe border.

"Are camels this big?" Carli asked.

Buck nodded his head. "I think so."

They both turned to see a pickup truck and livestock trailer pulling into Carli's driveway. Crazy Vera, her neighbor, waved at them.

"Hey, Vera." Carli waved back.

"I think I found everything you needed," she said.

Carli looked from Buck to Vera, and then walked to the back of the trailer as Vera unlatched the gate and swung it wide. Apparently, there was a conspiracy going on and Carli had been left out of the loop. Vera stepped up inside and came back out leading a little donkey.

"That's not stone-resin," exclaimed Carli.

"What's all this?" asked Lank as he came striding across the yard.

"Buck found us a Nativity, and part of it is alive."

"All right!" Lank showed as much enthusiasm as Buck, and Carli couldn't help but wonder what other creatures Vera might lead out of her trailer. But she had to admit, that donkey was the cutest little thing she'd ever seen. Carli scratched his head.

"I'll bring several bales of hay," Lank said. "What else ya got in there, Vera?"

The nephews suddenly burst out of the front door and made a beeline to the little donkey.

"March right back inside and get your coats, please." Carli pointed her finger at the house. "And then you can help us set up the manger."

Vera went back into the trailer and brought out a snow-white goat and baby lamb that bleated a greeting. Carli had to "Oooh" and "Aaah" over each one and pet them. By that time the boys were back and were assigned a spot to stand and hold lead ropes.

"Carli, I brought sumthin' special just for you."

Curious to figure out what Vera might be talking about, Carli walked closer to the end of the trailer. Inside, Vera unlatched the middle gate and behind it stood a huge muscular black bull.

"Maverick!" Carli exclaimed as she stepped closer to the trailer. "Come here, boy." Right after she had moved to Texas, she had taken over the care of a bottle calf whose mother was killed by coyotes. That sweet, little calf had grown into a one-thousand-pound bull, and Vera had bought him from Carli for her herd.

Buck and Lank grappled with the Holy Family, a kneeling shepherd, three Wise Men, and a life-size angel with a wingspan of over five feet. The last thing to put in place was the wooden manger, but one side of it had boards loose.

"We're taking this to the shop to repair and we'll be back," said Lank. Carli gave them a wave and turned to help Vera with the animals.

Vera and Carli arranged the statues with the Holy Family in the middle. They scattered hay everywhere and placed the animals on the outside of the scene tied to stakes.

"Boys," Vera said. "I have a very important job for you. Several times this afternoon, I need you to fill this bucket of water and take it to the animals and give them a drink. Can I count on you to do that?"

Junior and Zane nodded their heads, eyes wide from the importance of the task set before them. In a few more minutes, Buck and Lank unloaded the wooden manger. They all worked to spread hay under it, and then moved the Holy Family back under the shelter. To finish the display, Lank placed several battery-powered spotlights in the yard. Carli stepped out into the road to admire their work.

It was just beautiful. The perfect centerpiece for the celebration. Even though they had no electricity, things were coming together even better than she ever imagined.

Chapter Forty-Nine

Taylor

Taylor held the half-curtain aside and looked out through the kitchen window. Karissa came alongside and he draped an arm around her. The weather announcer's voice on the satellite radio described the ice storm and high winds that had descended on the area. Powerlines were down all over. Typical of Texas Panhandle weather, it would be completely different tomorrow.

"I don't think we'll get much accumulation," Taylor said. "And as pretty as it looks, I'll bet the roads are a real nightmare."

The announcer said, "Better to stay home and not risk the slippery roads."

Karissa fixed a cup of tea with honey. "Gee, I hate for the weather to mess up Carli's Open House. Do you think people will still come?"

"Maybe. Most have four-wheel drive. But on ice, that doesn't help." Taylor munched on chips.

"What about Hud?" she sipped her tea.

"I told him he could ride with us to the Wild Cow. Then when it's time, we can try to make it to Shayla's party. Or you can stay at the Wild Cow, and I'll risk the drive."

"And what are her plans?" Karissa asked.

"She's determined to get to her work party. I'm concerned about her being on the roads, especially at night by herself. But I haven't been able to talk any sense into her. You might have better luck."

"I don't know about that. She can be stubborn like someone else I know." Karissa fluttered her eyelashes at him. "But I don't mind since you look so handsome in your green plaid shirt. Very Christmassy, sir."

He gave her a little kiss.

Pounding footsteps from upstairs produced Hud in the kitchen. The broken arm had not slowed him down very much.

"Hey! So, when do we leave?"

"Later this afternoon," Taylor said.

Hud went right to the fridge. "Good. I can grab something to eat."

"Of course you can." Taylor grinned.

"We've been nibbling on that roast beef," Karissa said. "Why don't you make yourself a sandwich? I can help since you're one-armed."

"Sounds good to me." Their son towered over his mother and was an inch or so taller than his dad.

"Hud, so you're going to stay at the Wild Cow until we come back from Shayla's party to pick you up, right?" Taylor asked.

In between chews, Hud said, "Yeah. I'll try to help them clean up or something."

Karissa's eyes twinkled. "And maybe eat up, too? They'll have loads of goodies."

"Mmm, huh." Hud gave a big grin with his full

mouth.

Shayla entered the kitchen looking like a model from a winter catalog—cashmere scarf tied around her neck, knitted hat adjusted just so with her hair trailing down. Heavy corduroy skinny pants tucked into knee-high boots.

"Are you wearing that silk underwear that I gave you?" asked Karissa.

"Yes, I am. Thank you, Mama." Make up was just so. She carried a big tote, designer no doubt, and her furry gloves.

"You look nice, honey," her mom said.

"I got a text that because of the weather people were dressing down. No fancy dresses and heels, but I still have to go in to work today."

"That's probably a good idea, honey." Karissa softly smiled. "I still wish you weren't going by yourself. The roads might be dangerous."

"The roads are black ice, Shayla. That means you can't tell if they are slick or not. Just drive slow." Taylor gave her a kiss on the forehead.

Shayla put on her jacket. "I'll be careful. And I want to pick up my Christmas bonus for sure."

"Remember, no Christmas cheer before or at the party since you're driving." Taylor's face was serious.

"Oh, Dad, really."

"I'm just saying."

"Well, goes for you and Mom, too," Shayla said. "Carli might have spiked eggnog."

Karissa shook her head. "I don't think so. Cookies and hot chocolate."

Taylor faced Shayla, looked straight into her eyes, and rested his hands on her shoulders. "Honey, please be careful. We're going to be worried about you on the road."

"Dad, it's not even that far, for goodness sakes. What? About twenty, thirty minutes?"

"Even so. You call if you need anything at all," Taylor said. "We're just going to the Wild Cow for a little bit to help out. Then we'll try our best to get to your store by seven. Okay?"

"Sure, Dad. But you don't have to."

"We want to be with you, sweetie," he said. "We just wish everyone could be in the same place."

"All right. I've got to get going."

Everyone exchanged kisses and hugs, but Taylor still felt disconnected in some ways from his daughter.

Then Shayla left through the garage and took off in her vehicle.

Karissa touched her forehead. "I hate that she's going alone. I hope she'll be okay."

"Don't worry, darlin'. We'll see her before too long. We can follow her home after her party, on our way to pick up Hud."

Taylor saw the worry still filling Karissa's eyes, but he was at a loss as to how to alleviate it at the moment.

All he could do was pray for protection and reconciliation.

Chapter Fifty

Mandy

With sweaty palms and trembling knees, Mandy rapped gently on the door of her childhood home. Phin stood beside her, a protective hand on the small of her back.

"Coming," the soft, melodic voice of her mother called out just before the door was swung open.

Lerlene Milam froze before them, every hair in place, trim nails, perfect makeup. She never wore white after Labor Day, and her purse, belt, and shoes most certainly had to match. Mandy always thought that her mother had been born in the wrong era. Lerlene looked from one and then the other without saying a word.

"Mother," said Mandy.

Only silence, her lips pursed together in a thin line.

Phin removed his cowboy hat. "Hello, Mrs. Milam. I'm Phineas Shelton, but you can call me Phin. May we come in?"

"I suppose," she muttered, never taking her eyes off Phin and avoiding Mandy.

Tears welled up in Mandy's eyes as she walked past her mother. She missed her more than she would ever admit to anyone. With wooden legs, she allowed Phin to guide her to the sofa where they sat, and he balanced his hat on one knee. Growing up they rarely used the living room, particularly after her father had died. Lerlene sat in a rocking chair, crossing her legs at the ankle and clasping her hands in her lap.

"The tree looks nice," Mandy said. Her mother had decorated a tabletop tree that sat in the front picture window. Mandy recognized some of the ornaments that she had made in grade school.

"Mrs. Milam, we don't want to take up your time, but I'm here to ask you if I can have your daughter's hand in marriage."

Surprise flittered across her mother's face. "She doesn't live here. She can do whatever she wants."

"I understand, but I wanted to introduce myself. And I, uh we, would like for you to meet my parents. They are anxious to meet Mandy's family. We want your blessing. We want you to be a part of our lives."

Shock washed over her mother's face as her mouth dropped open. "Is this true, Mandy?"

"Yes, Mother. Phin is teaching me about forgiveness and love. I've grown up, and I'm trying to learn about real faith. You and I said horrible things to each other, but I'm hoping we can move forward. I just want to say I'm sorry."

Stubbornness and pride burned in her mother's eyes. This was not going to be easy, and Mandy regretted her decision to come here. Her mother avoided Mandy and glared at Phin instead. "You're not the father of this baby. He has another family.

My daughter had an affair with a married man."

"I didn't know he was married," Mandy said. "You have to believe me. Apparently, everyone knew but me."

"I tried to tell you." Mrs. Milam pursed her lips and stared straight ahead.

"Yes, you did. I was in love and too stubborn to listen. I didn't want to believe anything about him. In my eyes, he was perfect. I was wrong. That wasn't real love, Mother. I know that now."

Phin cleared his throat. "I am well aware of your daughter's situation, but that is in the past now. We've all made mistakes and bad choices, Mrs. Milam. But God forgives and so should you. The only thing that matters now is that I love your daughter and we are planning a future together. You can accept that or not."

Mandy's heart caught in her throat as she watched her mother. They may be tossed out on their ear at any minute. She couldn't be prouder of Phin. He certainly didn't mince words. Having him by her side gave her courage to continue.

"You may think of it as a mistake, but I will be welcoming a son in a few weeks. I'm going to be a mother. You're going to be a grandmother. That is the most perfect blessing that came out of one of the most horrible experiences in my life. And then I met Phin. Now I know what mature love is."

The mother looked at Mandy and then at Phin. "How did you meet?"

"We met at the sale barn. I still work there." Mandy cleared her throat. "The truth is we haven't known each other that long, but this is real. I know it."

Lerlene looked down at her lap. Her hands trembled. She glanced up with a quivering chin and a tear slowly ran down her face.

"Can you ever forgive me?" she murmured. "I did say some horrible things, but you ripped my heart out when you moved. First, we lost your father. And then you left me all alone. Why didn't you stay? We could have talked it out."

"I realize that now, Mom. Adults stay and work things out, but I was a stupid, selfish young girl who thought she knew everything."

"Yes, you are very stubborn. You get that from your father."

"The most important thing now is that I want this baby boy to know his grandmother."

"You're having a boy?" Lerlene put a hand over her mouth to stifle the sob that followed.

"Yes, and I'm thinking about naming him after dad, if it's all right with Phin." Mandy smiled at her mother.

"I think we should pray," said Phin. "Let's join hands."

If the situation hadn't been so serious and emotional, Mandy would have busted out laughing at the look on her mother's face when Phin grabbed her hand and bowed his head.

"Dear Lord, we come to you at this critical moment. We ask that you fill the hearts of this mother and daughter with forgiveness and love. Amen."

"That wasn't very long," said Lerlene.

"I don't believe in wasting God's time. I think people should shoot straight with Him and get to the point. He has so many other things he'd gotta deal with."

"I couldn't agree more, young man. You have my blessing." Lerlene smiled.

"There's something else you should know, Mama." Mandy scooted to the edge of the couch and leaned closer. "Phin's father married us yesterday. I hope you can be happy for me."

Phin grabbed her left hand and pushed it out for Lerlene to see. "This was my grandmother's ring. I'm sorry we didn't tell you right away, but I really did want your blessing. Thank you."

Mandy looked at her husband and realized that she fell more and more in love with him every day.

"We are on our way to the Wild Cow Ranch Open House, if you'd like to join us."

"I had planned to ride with some of my friends but let me call them and tell them I'll meet them there." A proper, but big, smile overtook her face.

"That would be fine, ma'am. Take however much time you need."

"In the meantime, why don't I make a pot of coffee? And would you like a slice of pecan pie before we go?"

"You made a pie?" Mandy stood straight up and clapped her hands. The news almost brought tears to her eyes. "My mama makes the best pecan pie in the state, and I'm not lying. I've really missed your cooking."

"It happens to be my favorite, so yes, I would definitely eat a piece of your pie." Phin stood and followed the ladies to the kitchen.

Lerlene filled the coffee pot and turned to look at them. The sudden tears that flowed down her face made Mandy cry too. They fell into each other's arms and hugged and cried and hugged some more.

Chapter Fifty-One

Taylor

Three of the Millers bundled up with their jackets, gloves, scarves, and hats and piled into Taylor's truck, Hud in the backseat. Karissa had also packed blankets and a thermos of hot chocolate in case the weather turned worse and they got stuck on the road.

Typical of the weather that could turn on a dime, the afternoon sun came out and burned bright and clear melting most of the thick ice that had swept in during the night.

Pulling up to the Wild Cow in late afternoon they saw red bows decorating all the fences. It looked quite festive against the thin layer of snow on the ground. "Look how pretty," Karissa said.

As Taylor parked his truck and everyone got out, they saw Buck approaching on an ATV. He stopped when he saw them.

"What are you carrying, Buck?" Taylor asked.

"Lanterns. Luminaries, Carli calls them. Power's out. None of the Christmas lights on the fences work. We've got about an hour to put all these out."

"We'll help." Taylor nodded to Hud.

"Sure," said his son. "I still have one good arm."

"I'll go in the cookhouse. See what the ladies need help with." Karissa squeezed Taylor's strong arm clothed in his warm canvas jacket.

"Where did you find all this stuff?" asked Taylor. "They look old."

"Carli found them in the basement along with the candles. I remember Jean using these before, but I didn't realize just how many she had."

For the next twenty minutes or so Buck, Taylor, and Hud added a hundred or more lanterns next to the fence and lined the roadway.

"Can we light them now?" Hud asked. "Otherwise, we'll have to make a second trip around."

"It's not dark yet," Buck said. "I don't want the wicks to run out before the people come."

"Do you think anybody will show up?" Taylor asked.

"Of course they'll come," Buck's voice was strong. "The town has been looking forward to this for some time. I think the front has moved on, and besides, a little weather's not gonna keep them away. We're Texans, man." He held up a fist and grimaced playfully.

Just then they saw a vehicle coming up the drive. Then another and another.

"I think you were right, Hud," Buck said. "Let's light these suckers now as we go. They'll last. I've got a few of those long lighters in the ATV."

"How's it going, guys?" Carli said. "Oh, hey, Taylor. Hud. Thanks so much for coming."

"Of course," Taylor said. "Glad to help. So, no power anywhere?"

"Lank got the generator going so we have electricity to the cookhouse, thank goodness," she said. "I don't think people would like cold chocolate drinks very much. Except maybe the kids. We'll just hang around the bonfire and enjoy the fellowship."

"Well, don't worry," Taylor said. "It'll all work out."

"I know it will. Somehow, I'm not that upset. It's been a crazy few weeks. But now I'm just going with the flow. Whatever happens, happens. It's in God's hands."

"Good attitude." Taylor smiled. "Carli, I just wanted to remind you although we mentioned it before. Karissa and I are going to stay as long as we can for the Open House, but we'll have to watch our time so we can get to Shayla's work party. I hope you don't mind."

"No, of course not. I appreciate your coming to the Open House. It means a lot to me."

Their heads turned as more pickups and cars were pulling into headquarters. Even a horse-drawn wagon with sleigh bells tinkling. Carli's excitement was almost child-like. "Another wagon! That is so beautiful."

"Yeah," Buck said. "Everyone is really getting into the Christmas spirit."

Carli placed a gloved hand on Taylor's arm. "Please tell your family thanks for helping. We really appreciate it. You be careful on the roads to the boutique party."

Another bundled figure came towards them. "You won't need to worry about that now."

Taylor squinted. "Shayla? Is that you? What are you doing here?" Was that his daughter shivering in her fashionable outfit?

"Well, I'm not Santa, but close enough." She chuckled. "I changed my mind and decided I wanted to be here instead. With all of you. With my family." She looked from Taylor to Carli. "I can always pick up my Christmas bonus when we go back to work after the holidays. And besides, I thought this party might need some music."

"Really? That's so thoughtful. Thank you, Shayla." Carli smiled at her half-sister.

"I borrowed a wireless speaker for my phone from a friend. I cued some Christmas music, and it plays really loud, too."

"Okay, then, Ms. D.J. I know the perfect spot where you can set up. Hit it!" Carli put an arm around Shayla, and they headed for one of the empty tables next to a refreshment table and positioned the music station.

When "White Christmas" played and Shayla said, "Sometimes the old music is my favorite," Carli couldn't contain her laugh.

"I couldn't agree with you more," she said.

Taylor followed the two young women and put a hand on Shayla's back. "I've got to ask you, why did you change your mind? You're missing your party."

"Well, half the time my boss is a real . . . you know what. And some of the others are, uh, kind of stuck up. I know I shouldn't say that, it being almost Christmas and all."

Taylor smiled. "It's okay. I think God'll forgive that. As long as you are sincere and nice to everybody you meet, and I know that that is the kind of person you are." Then he whispered into her ear. "And are you okay with Carli? Will you try to get to know her?"

Shayla gave Carli a genuine smile and said, "Well, Carli's not so bad. After all, she likes old Christmas music." They all chuckled. Then she looked at them with tears bubbling in her eyes. "Seriously," she said, "I don't want to be mad anymore. I don't think Carli is out to get me or take away my family." She looked at Carli and said, "You've been nice, and I've been kind of a brat. I'm sorry." Carli held out her arms and said, "It's okay, Shayla. I may not understand what it's like to be really close to a father, but I'm learning the importance of family. Let's just have a new beginning."

Then to her dad Shayla said, "I'm sorry, Dad. I know I've been a pain. I just couldn't help myself. It was all such a shock. I guess I had to get adjusted to the news of our family changing."

"But change can sometimes be a good thing, right?" Taylor said.

Carli still had a hand on Shayla's back and said, "I can tell you all kinds of stories about the twists and turns my life took. No mother, father, or family. I suddenly inherited a Texas ranch. And now look, I have a whole new family, and a husband to boot. And all these wonderful neighbors and townsfolk. I would have never imagined all of this. So yes, change can be very good, Shayla!"

Taylor embraced his daughter and held her tight. "I love you, Shayla."

Then he pulled Carli close to them and said to both women, "This has got to be the very best Christmas present I've ever had. Thank you both. I love you ladies." He was a little embarrassed that a tear was sneaking out of his eye. He brushed at it, cleared his throat.

Hud walked over and Shayla greeted him. "What in the world happened to your arm?"

He grinned. "All the cool kids have them. Where's yours? It's a real fashion statement. Didn't you know?"

As the kids drifted away to banter and argue like brothers and sisters do, Karissa walked up beside Taylor and put her arm through his.

"Shayla is here," he said.

"I see that."

"She wanted to be with her family. I know you're waiting to hear this, so I'll say it and get it out of the way. You were right."

She smiled up at her husband. "On occasion but remind me what I'm right about this time."

"You said to give her a chance and that she'd do the right thing." Taylor leaned down and left a kiss on her temple. "We raised some pretty darn good kids, didn't we?"

"Yes, dear, I believe we did."

"Let's go enjoy that big bonfire over there."

Chapter Fifty-Two

Carli

Carli watched the bonfire light bounce off the faces of her friends and neighbors as they sang "Silent Night". A soft glow illuminated Wild Cow Ranch headquarters from a few flashlights and cell phones. Her Grandma Jean's luminaries burned bright around the front porch and extended out into the yard and then spaced evenly on both sides of the road that bisected headquarters. Her heart warmed at the reverent voices. She stood silent, not singing, just listening.

On one side of her stood her husband, Lank, strumming his guitar, his deep voice rising in perfect pitch. On the other side, with his arm around her waist, stood Taylor Miller, her birth father. He had his other arm around the waist of her half-sister, Shayla. Karissa and her half-brother Hud were there too. What a surreal moment. In a million years she had never imagined that she would have ever found her birth father and be blessed with a new family too. Carli had both hands resting on a shoulder of each nephew in front of her.

Buck raised his arm after the song ended. "On behalf of all of us at the Wild Cow Ranch, I want to thank you for coming out here tonight on this chilly evening. Looks like the wind has died down which helps. We are honoring Ward and Jean, who I'm sure a lot of you remember. Their granddaughter Carli and her husband Lank are pleased to continue the tradition of inviting you all to an Open House."

Claps, whistles, and cheers followed.

"We've had more than our share of incidents recently. Lank's nephews with two broken arms. Taylor's son Hud showed up here with a broken arm." Buck chuckled. "Lola's sister Isabelle—one broken ankle, but in three places. Hopefully, my wife will be back in a few days. Thanks to the good Lord who will repair these breaks, and we pray He will return them to new without any lingering pain."

"Yes, Lord," someone said from the crowd.

"These accidents got me thinking. Aren't we all a little broken? Maybe not bones. But hearts. Or memories. Or sadness. Feelings of guilt, of not measuring up. Maybe not accepting change. Holding grudges. Humans are flawed. And frail. Look at how easy we can break our bones. Our feelings also can be broken just as easily."

Some voices in the crowd mumbled, "Yes."

"The good news is that God wants to heal us. He loves us like a good, good Father. This Christmas I pray it is a new beginning for all of us. Reach out to our Father and accept the greatest Christmas gift of all He is extending to us. Hold it in your hearts. Let go of the old and embrace the new. Love one another. Love our Creator. Merry Christmas, everyone!"

Voices joined in saying "Merry Christmas". Carli clapped and cheered too.

"Mom! Dad!" Junior shouted and ran into the arms of his mother.

"Y'all made it after all," said Lank as he hugged his sister.

"Yes, we saw that cold front moving in and decided to leave a few days early. We didn't want to be stuck in an airport somewhere." Kelly wrapped her arms around Junior again and planted a kiss on his forehead. "I sure missed you."

"I'm not certain where your youngest is, but he's around here somewhere," said Carli. "I am so happy to see you guys."

"We can't thank you and Lank enough for keeping the boys. We had such a good time, and Matt got his promotion. He worked really hard and made a good impression."

"I'm glad to hear it. His promotion doesn't mean a move, does it?" Carli frowned a little.

"Oh no. I think it means a bigger office. We're staying in Amarillo."

"There is something that Lank needs to tell you." Carli glared at her husband, who paled when his sister looked his way.

"If this is about broken arms, we got an email from Junior," Kelly said.

"You did? Junior, why didn't you tell me you were emailing your mother?" Carli laughed. "All that nagging my husband every day for nothing. You already knew."

"Sorry, Sis. I didn't know how to tell you," Lank said.

"We'll definitely need to have a talk before we leave the boys with you again," Matt said with a deep frown on his face.

Lank's eyes grew wide with guilt as he looked at his brother-in-law.

Matt slapped him on the shoulder and then laughed. "Got ya, bro."

Carli turned in the direction of a tap on her arm.

Mandy smiled at her and said, "I'd like you to meet my mother."

"Mrs. Milam, it's so nice to meet you. I'm glad you all could be here." Carli shook hands and exchanged pleasantries.

And then to Mandy, she said, "And I'm glad to see you looking so well."

"I feel really good today. Better than I have felt in several weeks. I have so much energy today for some reason," Mandy said. "And this is my husband, Phin."

"What? When did y'all get married?" Carli hugged them both. "I'm so happy you found each other."

"Phin's father married us yesterday afternoon. His parents are so nice."

Carli leaned close and gave Mandy another squeeze.

"Oww," said Mandy.

"Oh, I'm so sorry. I didn't mean to hurt you." Carli backed away. Mandy's face suddenly turned ghost white and she bent over, grabbed her stomach, and moaned.

"I think she's going into labor!" Mrs. Milam said. "Phin. Bring your truck around fast. Let's get this girl to the hospital. I'm about to become a grandmother!"

Phin took off in a dead run. The crowd parted and several people supported Mandy on either side and walked her towards the road.

As Carli watched, Crazy Vera, one of her fence line neighbors, came and stood beside her. "This was by far the best Open House I've ever been to."

"Vera! So good to see you. Thanks for coming."

"I wouldn't have missed it for anything, Carli. Unless maybe I had broken a bone or sumthin'." Then Vera gave a booming belly laugh.

Carli's heart warmed at all the kind words she had received from the townsfolk who had come out for the Wild Cow's "new/old" Christmas tradition. Carli continued reflecting on the heartwarming scene before her. Maybe happiness wasn't about the hype of Christmas or having electricity, although that would have been nice. Maybe real happiness was about the small moments in life. Time spent with the boys shopping for mac and cheese and drinking hot chocolate at Belinda's coffee shop. Or digging through a basement full of memories. Or baking cookies with Lola.

"What are you thinking about?" asked Taylor as he draped a hand over her shoulder.

"Oh, I'm thinking that it's not the big events in life that stay in your heart. It's the little moments that leave a much bigger impression."

"You are so right," said her father. "Like a baby coming into the world." They both watched as several people helped Mandy into Phin's truck, the cab light reflecting the excitement on their faces contrasted by the pain on Mandy's face as she clutched her stomach.

Carli shook her head as tears spilled from her eyes. She swiped one cheek with a gloved hand.

"I feel cheated that I never got to hold you as a baby, that I never even knew you existed. But I am so thankful we get to have a second chance," Taylor said.

Carli could only nod her head. His words meant more than he would ever know.

She thought of every single person in her life and how much she loved them. God had really been good to her, and she was truly grateful.

"I know you didn't get to have the ranch head-quarters lit up like you wanted, but I think it's been a fun event. We've had more than one hundred people show up." Lank put an arm around Carli's shoulders. "You did good."

"The bonfire has really been fun, and the lumi-naries look so beautiful. Thank you for playing the guitar too." Carli snuggled closer under his arm. "Sometimes the quietest moments are the loudest in your heart."

Acknowledgements

Many thanks to the teachers who encouraged my writing journey. At an early age when choosing an elective in school, I was enamored with the word "journalism". I wasn't quite sure what the study or profession entailed but the word was so nice, kind of long (unlike "art"), a little mysterious, and for some reason it called to me as though God was lighting my path.

Dorothy Massey, my journalism teacher for grades 9th through 12th in Miami, Florida—She gave us extra credit for just writing. For that lesson she emphasized quantity over quality (later for the school paper it would be quality). Mrs. Massey said, "Just write." My Dad laughed and was amazed that I had invented a story about how the nail on the wall felt about holding up the picture.

Peg O'Connor, my communications professor at Reinhardt College in Waleska, Georgia—I completed my bachelor's degree later in life and "followed" Peg by taking every communications course she taught. That was another springboard for my writing career. Plus, I gained such a wonderful friendship with Peg. I miss her and hope our paths cross again.

The professors at Kennesaw State University in Kennesaw, Georgia taught me a great deal through the M.A.P.W. (professional writing) program. It was also an honor to be immersed in the group of writers who were my fellow students. I hope they are all doing wonderful things now.

And, of course, I thank God for giving me the gift of writing; my extraordinary co-author and friend Natalie Bright; the Western Writers of America; Wolfpack Publishing and CKN Christian Publishing; and so many others.

Denise F. McAllister

A Look At:
Everly by Kay P. Dawson

A SWEET, CLEAN, MAIL-ORDER BRIDE ROMANCE!

The terms of her father's will leave Everly with no choice but to marry before her 21st birthday to ensure the security of her family.

Will she be able to get over her anger towards men in enough time to find someone to marry?

Answering an ad for a mail-order bride, she finds Ben – a man who needs a woman to help him raise his two nieces left in his care. Can they find love while dealing with both a vindictive stepmother who wants to stop her from marrying, and a meddling woman who is determined to take the children from Ben? They will both have to learn to trust, even as the past threatens to ruin everything.

"Tangles of emotions, a little bit of suspense and then a happy ending! Everything to make a beautiful clean romance set in the old west!" – Reader

About the Author

Natalie Bright -

Natalie Bright writes stories that combine her passion for history of the American West and the unique people of the Texas Panhandle, where she calls home. She is a fifth generation Texan, and a fan of friendly people, a good story, Texas sunsets, and connecting with readers.

Follow Author Updates links above to read PRAIRIE PURVIEW, a Blog focusing on the amazing places and history of Texas, and the inspiration behind her work and featuring her photography.

THE WILD COW RANCH SERIES (CKN/ Wolfpack Publishing)

Find Natalie on Instagram @natsgrams, Pinterest, LinkedIn, and Facebook as NatalieBrightAuthor. If you like cows, the Texas sky, and all things Western, then you're in the right place.

Denise F. McAllister-

Lovers of the West can be born in the most unlikely of places. For Denise F. McAllister, her start was in Miami, Florida, surrounded by beaches and the Everglades.

But the marvels of television transported her to stories of the West—Bonanza, Gunsmoke, The Virginian, and many others—that she fondly recalls watching with her brother every Saturday morning.

After being in the working world for some years, Denise F. McAllister applied her life experience to study for degrees in communications and professional writing. She loved going back to college later in life and hardly ever skipped a class as in her younger years.